was born in Harrow in 1893. As a student of music she became interested in research in the music of the fifteenth and sixteenth centuries, and spent ten years of her life as one of the four editors of the ten-volume compilation *Tudor Church Music*. In 1925 she published her first book of verse, *The Espalier*. With the publication of the novels *Lolly Willowes* in 1926, *Mr Fortune's Maggot* and *The True Heart* in the two following years, she achieved immediate recognition. The short stories she contributed to the *New Yorker* for over forty years established her reputation on both sides of the Atlantic.

In 1927 Sylvia Townsend Warner visited New York as guest critic for the *Herald Tribune*. In the 1930s she was a member of the Executive Committee of the Association of Writers for Intellectual Liberty and was a representative for the Congress of Madrid in 1937, thus witnessing the Spanish Civil War at first hand.

In all, Sylvia Townsend Warner has published seven novels, five volumes of poetry, a volume of essays, nine volumes of short stories, and an acclaimed biography of T. H. White.

A novelist of formidable imaginative power, each of Sylvia Townsend Warner's novels is a new departure, ranging from the revolutionary Paris of 1848 in *Summer Will Show* (1936), a fourteenth-century Abbey in *The Corner That Held Them* (1943) to the South Seas Island of *Mr Fortune's Maggot*, and nineteenth-century rural Essex in *The True Heart*. Virago publish the latter two novels and also her delightful collection of Gilbert White's writings about his tortoise, Timothy, which she edited and introduced in *The Portrait of a Tortoise* (1946).

THE
TRUE HEART

by

SYLVIA TOWNSEND

WARNER

To
My Mother
Who first told me a story

Published by VIRAGO PRESS Limited 1978
Ely House, 37 Dover Street, London W1X 4HS

Reprinted 1981

First published 1929 by Chatto & Windus Limited

Copyright © Susanna Pinney & William Maxwell 1978,
Executors of the Estate of Sylvia Townsend Warner

Printed in Great Britain by litho at
The Anchor Press, Tiptree, Essex

British Library Cataloguing in Publication Data
Warner, Sylvia Townsend
    The true heart. — (Virago modern classics)
    I. Title
    823'.912[F]   PR6045.A812
    ISBN 0-86068-048-7

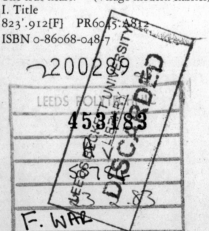

deal of ingenuity on the Victorian versions of
the divine characters, disguising their names and
abilities. Mrs Seaborn was the sea-born Venus,
Mrs Oxey, Juno the patron of marriage (it was
an axiom of that date that only by the provision
of brothels could modest women retain their
virtue); the apple-woman and Mrs Disbrowe
are Demeter. Queen Victoria is Persephone.
These disguises were so efficient that no reviewer
saw what I was up to. Only my mother recognised the basis of the story.

Sylvia Townsend Warner, Dorset, 1978

PREFACE

In July 1922, in the stationery department of Whiteley's I saw some ordnance maps, and bought one of Essex, because I didn't know Essex even by map. The green marsh on the map pleased me, and the blue creeks, and the marsh names. On August Bank Holiday I went to Southend, took a bus out of town to a name on my map and spent a long slow day walking about. I came to a creek running slowly, and beyond it was an island with a white house on it and some farm buildings. This was the genesis of *The True Heart*. Later that summer I went, again by map, to Drinkwater St Lawrence, stayed there, at a small farm and spent a month in the marshes, walking and exploring. All the landscape of *The True Heart* comes from those rambles.

Two years later (I had begun *Lolly Willowes* then) I began thinking enough about writing to say to Bea Howe that it would be a good exercise to take a folk-song or a fairy story, and retell it. This was the basis of *Eleanor Barley* (a folk-song) and the retelling of the tale of Cupid and Psyche from Apuleius in *The True Heart*: I spent a great

THE TRUE HEART

Part i

I T was the 27th of July 1873, and prize-giving day
at the Warburton Memorial Female Orphanage. Mr Warburton, the son of the foundress,
had come to give away the prizes. He sat under
the shade of an evergreen behind a table covered
with a crimson cloth, and as each girl approached,
he rose and took up the prize indicated to him
by Miss Pocock, the Matron. Holding it in his
large, white, gentleman's hands, he spoke of the
pleasure it gave him to reward merit, and to en-
courage an institution so interesting to his family;
then, with a slight bow, he gave the prize to the
curtseying girl, and sat down again, amidst applause from the lady patronesses and the female
orphans, who sat grouped around him, the lady
patronesses in the shade and the female orphans
in the sun.

It was extremely hot. The patronesses un-
buttoned their kid gloves and fanned themselves,
and as girl followed girl, Mr Warburton's words
of commendation became more and more frag-
mentary, and the gesture with which he handed
over the prize suggested not so much bestowal as
disencumbrance. This sort of thing was not in

his line. He but did it to honour his mother's memory, and while he spoke of merit and application, he could not help thinking how in little more than a fortnight's time he would be shooting over a Scotch grouse moor, and wondered if it would be as hot as this, and if the birds would be plentiful. It certainly could not be hotter. Only Miss Pocock bore the heat without flinching. She lived for the glories of this day when every prize redounded to her honour, was in truth presented to her, though its outward seeming was diverted to one or other of her charges. She had been up since 4 A.M. putting finishing touches to the orphans' housewifery. Now she wore her new purple bodice and her face of state, where the expression never varied, as if her countenance were cased up in invisible stays.

For the fifth time the same girl approached the table, and the applause of the lady patronesses swelled into quite a little pattering storm. Sukey Bond had gained three prizes and two certificates: she was a credit to the institution.

'Prize for good conduct,' Mr Warburton read out, 'awarded to Sukey Bond. A copy of Bunyan's *Holy War*. With illustrations, I see. Sukey Bond, I have great pleasure in presenting you with the prize for good conduct. Er—conduct is everything.'

She took the prize and curtseyed. He could only see the top of her head, but that seemed vaguely familiar to him.

'Haven't I seen you before?' he inquired. Such unexpectedly conversational accents arrested all the fans. Miss Pocock leant forward and whispered something.

'*Five* winners!' he murmured. 'Clear starching and the Lord knows what!'

The girl's head and shoulders had now risen again above the table, and Mr Warburton surveyed the prodigy with interest.

'Odd little crow!' was his inward comment. 'All eyes and bones. Mother a French ballet-dancer. Queer enough pack they've got here, I daresay.'

At a gesture from Miss Pocock, Sukey remained standing where she had risen from her curtsey. Mr Warburton resumed the god.

'It is very gratifying to learn that you have made such good use of your opportunities. Youth's the season—er—to remember thy Creator, and fit yourself to be a useful member of society. I hope you will continue to do so.'

Every feeling orphan felt for Sukey Bond, so to be hauled back again and preached at, and to have to perform her curtsey twice over. Even Miss Pocock emitted a sustaining smile. But

Sukey was too much wrought up to a sense of destiny to be embarrassed, and as she carried back the prize for good conduct and laid it down beside the dress-length of brown calico and the ivory thimble, her movements were slow and precise, and her face wore a preoccupied look. A feeling of solemnity isolated her from her surroundings, and a sense of unknown responsibilities weighted her steps with dignity ; for this resplendent day was the last of her days at the Warburton Memorial Female Orphanage ; to-morrow she was going out to service. A place had been found for her upon a farm in Essex. Her wages were to be ten pounds a year, and nothing more was required of her than honesty, industry, cleanliness, sobriety, obedience, punctuality, modesty, Church of England principles, good health and a general knowledge of house-work, dairywork, washing, mending, and plain cooking. It had all been arranged by Mrs Seaborn, the wife of the rector of Southend, and she was to make her journey to-morrow under the charge of this lady.

Mrs Seaborn was a lady patroness, and an especially notable one, being related to Mr Warburton. When Sukey stood before the approving half-circle she had wondered which of the silken skirts was Mrs Seaborn's ; but further her speculations had not risen, for she had not dared to lift her eyes and scan these ladies in the face.

Sukey Bond had spent five years at the orphanage. She came there at the age of eleven, a timid, under-grown child with a crooked back, for being the eldest of the family and the only girl it seemed that she had learnt to walk for no other purpose than to carry her brothers. When her mother died—but Mr Warburton was out in his pedigree, for Mrs Bond was a laundress and lived in Notting Dale—Sukey was prepared to take her place, to wash and dress the last baby, to cook and mend for the others. But this was not possible, for there was no bread-winner in the family, Mr Bond having gone off to the Irish to assuage his grief, broken his leg while in liquor, and died of gangrene. The parish authorities had to step in. The youngest Bond was adopted by the wife of a rich corn-chandler, and the others were bestowed in various charitable institutions.

Though her back grew straight again, Sukey regretted the warm burden that had stooped her to one side. For many nights she lay awake, quietly snuffling for her lost charges. They were lost to her indeed, for though she was now taught to write, the Warburton Memorial Female Orphans were allowanced to one penny stamp a fortnight, and the anxious letters that she sent, turn and turn about, to her five brothers, could not do much to hold the scattered family together. Sometimes an answer came, but it was only a slighter repetition of her own assurances and good wishes, as though a blank wall had tossed back to her a mutilated echo of her words.

At the orphanage her conduct was exemplary, but exemplary without mark. She learnt what she was taught, she did as she was bid, but for all this she was neither much praised by her superiors nor disliked by her fellows. Her one salient gift was a knack for obedience—a knack that amounted almost to a genius—and any creditable performance of hers, whether in fine darning, or short crust, or the kings of Israel and Judah, was accepted as the natural result of this obliging disposition.

Now all this was at an end, and her thoughts peered at the morrow. She knew nothing of the country save by hearsay, and all that she could forecast of her life on the farm was, that she would have to get up very early, and perhaps hold a basin at the pig-killings. Her notion of what the country looked like was coloured by religion—by a line in a hymn about fields that stood *dress'd in living green*, and by the painted window she looked at on Sunday, where the

Good Shepherd was shown conducting his flock through a landscape of very small fields intersected by narrow blue brooks.

But Miss Pocock had said that New Easter was in the marshes. That word cast a chill into her flesh. A marsh was damp, was wild, was dangerous. Bad airs wandered there, and stagnant pools reflected an angry sunset with a flare of blood. She thought of darkening evenings in autumn, the wind prowling in the hedge. From the green imaginary fields the sheep fled in panic, and she saw an encampment of gipsies, who kidnapped little children and ate viper's flesh.

So terrible did this seem to her that when, the last prize awarded and Mr Warburton's top hat having flashed past the railings at a brisk trot, Miss Pocock led her forward to meet Mrs Seaborn, she made up her mind to a desperate step— to beg that she might not be sent to New Easter. But raising her eyes to Mrs Seaborn's face she knew that this lady could only take her where it would be good for her to go. Mrs Seaborn's grey silk dress, as it swept over the lawn, seemed to sing a low tune. Her shoulders were rounded and drooping, her voice stroked the ear. She was like a dove, and the small onyx buttons on her dress were like doves' eyes.

When Mrs Seaborn turned away, Sukey felt as if she were being softly lowered out of a white cloud. At prayers that evening Miss Pocock asked God's protection for the girl who was going out into the world, even mentioning her by name. But this honour, almost amounting to a personal introduction, scarcely brushed Sukey's consciousness, for all her thoughts were set on the morrow, when she would see this harmonious creature again.

She had never been for a railway journey, but she forgot to look at the smoke coming out of the engine, she forgot to watch the house-tops jostling by, she forgot to eat her sandwiches. She did nothing but gaze at Mrs Seaborn, and this she might do without impertinence, for Mrs Seaborn leaned back with closed eyes and a gentle expression, holding upon her lap a fine handkerchief and a flask of smelling-salts.

Sukey wished that she could stay with her for ever. She would work night and day and ask for no wages, for to serve such a mistress would be wages enough. She framed the request in her mind, feeling sure that her wish would be understood and granted. But while Mrs Seaborn looked so peaceful, almost indeed as if she were asleep, she could not be rude enough to disturb her, and when at last she spoke, it was to bid

Sukey gather up her things, since they were at Southend.

They drove to the rectory, where Sukey was sent into the kitchen to have a cup of tea. The kitchen walls were hung with shining instruments: she guessed that they had to do with cooking, but their uses were unknown to her. Seeing them, she remembered her wish to be a servant to Mrs Seaborn, and was abashed at it. An hour ago, with the train whirling her past fields and cottage roofs and under the brief roar of bridges, such a wish, such a fate had not seemed too exalted. But now the inspiration of movement was taken away, and sitting very still and looking at the shining instruments and at the five jelly-moulds like temples which were ranged along the mantelpiece, she knew that she had no place in this splendour. It was all too high, too intricate for her.

A rattle of wheels was heard in the stable-yard. The cook said :

' I expect that is Mr Noman come to fetch you. You 'd better carry out your traps.'

Sukey obeyed. In the middle of the stable-yard was a dovecot on a green pole. When they heard her tin box grating over the cobbles, the doves flew out, flapping their wings as though they were impatient of this disturbance. Sukey sat down on her box to wait. Beyond the brick wall was a row of lime-trees. Their blossom was faded, it hung down limp and tarnished, but it still sent out a sweet monotonous odour. Within the house she could hear the sounds of washing-up and the voices of the servants talking at the sink, but the yard was silent. Sometimes Mr Noman's horse struck its forefoot against the cobbles, and sometimes a dove flew from one branch to another with a clattering flight. Sukey felt that she would remember the rectory stable-yard all her life long. A sorrow so pure that it was almost peace welled up in her bosom. She forgot that she was on her way to New Easter; she could only think how much she loved Mrs Seaborn and that now she must part from her.

Presently Mrs Seaborn came into the yard with Mr Noman. Mr Noman was tall and bulky, his great girth intimidated her. She had but a con-fused impression of his upper part; but he wore leather gaiters and his legs looked reliable, and when he addressed her his voice was loud and benevolent. She climbed up into the front seat and the trap creaked and swayed as he fol-lowed her.

Sukey could not turn her head as they drove out of the yard. Her thoughts nursed Mrs Sea-born's parting words of admonition, and staring at the bobbing rump of the horse in front of her she vowed to be worthy of Mrs Seaborn's trust, and to do her duty in that state of life to which it had pleased God to call her. Thinking of this, she took off her black cotton gloves and rolled them into a ball. Her eyes were painful with unshed tears. She did not notice the streets of Southend, nor the dusty elms that drooped over the road when it came out into the fields. They drove in silence till Mr Noman pointed northeastward with his whip and said :

' There are the marshes.'

They had reached the brow of a little rise, and before them the fields sloped downward and away to rich-coloured flats, streaked and dotted with glittering water. Here and there were farmsteads, and a few groups of dwarfish trees showed up black and assertive, at odds with the solitude. Not a shadow fell on the marsh from the cloudless sky, nothing moved there ; even the cattle were still, clustered round the trees for shade. It lay in unstirring animation, stretched out like the bright pelt of some wild animal. To the eastward a dark rim bounded it, and beyond this was a further expanse that shone, baffling the eye.

' Is that the sea ? ' she asked.

' No,' answered Mr Noman. ' Those are the

saltings. The sea's away beyond. The tide will have turned by now,' he added after a pause. ' Presently the sea will come in.'

She wondered how far the sea would come, and if it ever came far enough to surround the farm-steads, so that with their tarred sides they would look like the Noah's Ark on the matchboxes.

The road grew rougher as it left the hedges behind and came out upon the marsh. Before long it became no more than a cart-track, and the horse fell into a walk. In front of them was a farm, with a walnut-tree growing beside it. Sukey asked if this were New Easter. Mr Noman shook his head. This was Ratten's Wick, he said; here they would leave the horse and trap, which he had borrowed from his brother-in-law be-cause his own nag had fallen lame. They passed through the rickyard, carrying the tin box be-tween them. Beyond the rickyard the track continued, small and grass-grown. It ran un-deviating through the marsh towards a high bank of earth. Here everything seemed to end, stemmed by this green barrier which reared up before them as they approached.

The flatness of the marsh throws out the sense of proportion. When they were come to the foot of the bank, Sukey was surprised to find that it was not more than fourteen or fifteen feet in height. Taking hold of the bushes that clothed its sides like a fleece, she scrambled to the top.

She uttered a cry of surprise at what she saw. Below her was a creek of slowly-running water that pushed its way inland over thick-stemmed grasses and tufts of sea-lavender. Beyond the creek was a low green shore, and not far from the water's edge was a farmhouse, made of wood, and tarred. An old white horse was standing in an enclosure. His head was thrust stiffly forward. He was asleep.

Mr Noman whistled. The old horse woke up, and a man came from an outhouse, shielding his eyes against the sun. When he saw Mr Noman he stepped down to the shore, and unloosing a shallow-bottomed boat he pulled across the creek to where they stood.

' This is the new girl, Zeph,' said Mr Noman.

' What do you think of Derryman's Island, Missy ? ' asked Zeph.

Sukey had learned from her geography book that an island is a piece of land surrounded on all sides by water. She had also learned about coral islands, whole islands made of the same stuff as Miss Pocock's brooch. If the dry mud of the New Easter landing-place had been a rose-coloured beach she could not have set foot on it with greater emotion, so wonderful was it to tread upon an island.

Next morning a sea-fog covered the marsh. Looking from her window, she could see nothing but the tops of the farm buildings emerging from the vapour, their mouse-coloured thatch flushed in the sunrise. There was no wind, yet the vapour was stirred with innumerable small eddies that circled and dissolved in strange soundlessness. Animals moved in the fog ; she could hear them tearing up the grass and blowing out their breath. Overhead the sky was perfectly blue. She forgot to be disappointed that she could see so little of her new surroundings. She had dreamed of them, she now remembered, but nothing could please her better than this waking, like waking up into a dream.

It was not till breakfast was finished and the men gone out to work that the mist cleared off suddenly, like a veil twitched out of sight. She ran out of doors to enjoy, if only for a minute, the glittering freshness of the morning. A mild air breathed over the fields, bringing with it the smell that is peculiar to the marshes—part smell of warm inland earth, part smell of the sea, melancholy as a desire—the smell of the marriage of two elements. The noise of grasshoppers was everywhere ; there seemed to be one for each tuft of grass, so loud and incessant was their concert.

A feeling came over her that she was being watched, and ashamed to be caught idling on her first morning she turned towards the house. A young woman stood by the door, eyeing her keenly. She was tall and strapping, and her face was sunburnt.

' I suppose you are the new girl ? '

Her voice was loud enough to traverse the distance between them. Sukey's was not. She nodded and approached the stranger.

' My name 's Prudence Gulland. I was girl here before you, and Mr Noman told me to come over and learn you the ways of the place.'

There seemed to be a great deal to impart. With loud slapping movements and bewildering activity Prudence darted from one household task to another, and as she worked she kept up a running fire of cautions and admonitions, Sukey being bidden to follow her round and attend.

' That 's the woodhouse,' said Prudence, opening a door into a speckled obscurity and shutting it again with a bang. ' Full of bats. They 'll catch hold of your hair if you don't look out. . . . Never touch Mr Noman's gun. It 'll go off. . . . Mind you don't slip in this puddle when you 're carrying out the swill. And be careful of that drake. He 's artful.'

As the morning wore on, Sukey began to be depressed. There was a dreadful cordiality in Prudence's warning words. Presently to warning she added condolence, cordial also.

' I can see you 'll never stand the winter. You 'll be moped to death, coming from London, and you such a dweeny specimen. Do you get chilblains ? '

' No.'

' You 'll get them here. All the marsh-folk has them. Agues, too. And no doubt you 'll take them worse, being a stranger. Whatever made you come to the marsh ? '

' I was sent here. Mrs Seaborn arranged it.'

' Oh, Mrs Seaborn did, did she ? '

Prudence's tone was unpleasant. Sukey fired up instantly.

' I think Mrs Seaborn is a lovely lady.'

' Well, my goodness gracious me, there 's no need to be such a spitfire. I never said she wasn't, did I ? But I can tell you, whoever sent you here, you won't like it, and that 's a fact. It 's as doleful as an empty church. And colder.'

Sukey wondered if she should ask about the Nomans, but Prudence forestalled her, casting the same lurid gleam upon them as upon everything else at New Easter.

'Cheerful company you 'll find them,' she exclaimed. 'They might be a pack of bears. The old man never speaks, and no more don't his sons. Young Eric 's a ninny. As for Zeph, he 's Peculiar. Lots of the marsh-folk are.'

'Why?'

'They don't go to church,' said Prudence gloomily, 'nor speak evil.'

Just before noon and dinner came Reuben, Mr Noman's eldest son. He did not come into the house, but walked to and fro between the tall rows of runner-beans. Presently he began to whistle. Prudence put on her hat and glanced round the kitchen to see if she had mislaid anything. Then she said:

'Mind you don't let on to the old man that I have been here.'

'I thought he told you to come.'

Prudence made a derisive noise against the roof of her mouth and ran from the kitchen. But at the door she paused and stared hard at Sukey, measuring her up and down, smiling and pursing her lips.

'So Mrs Seaborn sent you here, did she? Seems as if she 'd got quite a fancy for sending folks here. Wonderful took with the place she must be. Good as a rubbish-heap to her, I daresay.'

' Who else did . . . ? '

Prudence laughed and turned away. From the window Sukey saw her go down to the landing-place, and after a minute Reuben emerged from among the bean-rows and followed her, walking slowly and cutting at the rampion-heads with a stick, as though he found time heavy on his hands. Then she heard the sound of oars.

Sukey was deeply offended. The remark about the rubbish-heap she could have overlooked, for it was aimed at her, and it was clear that Prudence had taken as instant a dislike to her as she to Prudence; but to speak so disrespectfully of Mrs Seaborn—that was unpardonable. She said nothing of the morning's visit to Mr Noman, for though she knew she had been made a cat's-paw, she would not—so she said in her thoughts—demean herself by betraying the other. She tried to put it out of her mind; but all that afternoon the memory of Prudence accompanied her as she went about her work, baffling and discouraging her.

A trifle of laziness had gone to aid that decision not to demean herself; for Sukey had an easygoing streak in her nature and might have been inclined to let things slide if the circumstances of her life had allowed it. As things were, she directed a scrupulous industry to an ideal of idleness when she could sit in a neat perfected kitchen where nothing remained to do.

She would soon have settled down to her new life but for the uneasy turn which had been given to her thoughts by the episode of the first morning. Though her good sense told her to dismiss such feelings, Prudence's words had made her distrustful of her surroundings and inclined to pity herself. She had no grounds for self-pity. She was well housed and well fed—a great deal better fed than at the orphanage, where second helpings were not allowed except on boiled-rice day—the country air agreed with her, the work was within her power, and no one found fault, or interfered with her performance of it. Nor was she oppressed by the tedium with which Prudence had threatened her : within doors she was too busy to feel lonely, and when she went abroad she was too much excited by the strangeness of the landscape to be disconcerted by its austerity. But for all this, she could not shake off the feeling that her lot was in some way deplorable and fraught with menace.

Sometimes she attributed this uneasiness to living upon an island. At first the idea of an island was wholly delightful; it was almost an extension of the safe feeling of being tucked in bed. To this succeeded a fancy that those who live upon an island are exposed to a special unprotectedness. They are all alone, cut off from the succour, the homely example of the mainland. They are out of sight, out of mind. They exist but as in a dream.

This impression of leading a life insubstantial and dreamlike was strengthened when Sukey learned about the marsh. All these fields, Zeph told her, had been filched, acre by acre, from the sea. Within the hearsay of men living the sea had come up to within a mile of Dannie, which lay inland and northward of Derryman's Island, its church hidden in a grove of ash and ilex. Dyke after dyke had been built, thrusting back the weakening tide. Each farmer was responsible for the upkeep of the stretch of the sea-wall which guarded his property, and there was no greater crime in the marshes than to allow the wall to be broken down by cattle, for one tide flooding in through the breach might set back the work of reclamation for years. Once enclosed, the latest-won strip of saltings was ditched and channelled. A new tide swept over it, a tide of vegetation exulting in the gross soil. Another ten years, and the green waste was put under the plough and corn grew upon what had been the bed of the sea.

Zeph spoke with the animation of a conqueror, but Sukey took the sea's part, and so, she thought, did the marsh, for with the rising of the tide did not all the land-locked pools and channels swell in sympathy ? She remembered her first sight of the marsh, how it had lain outstretched and impassive, containing its secret longing for the hour when the sea-fog would come flowing over it, billowing in like the sea's ghost come back to claim its own. It was small wonder that the farm and the life she led there seemed tinged with unreality, small wonder that she felt astray from her proper self. It was dream-like indeed that she should be washing clothes and baking bread where once the fishes swam.

She hoped that Zeph would offer to take her to the sea, for though she knew that she had but to follow the windings of the creek eastward to find her way there by herself, she lacked courage to go alone. Herds of cattle and horses grazed over the marsh ; but she did not dread these, for she soon discovered that the worst they did was to follow her, snorting and inquisitive, but not intending her any harm. It was the sea itself that she dreaded. The Bible had taught her that the sea was to be feared. Storms arose there, the cruel floods clapped their hands. Perhaps a wave would take hold of her and bear her away, or perhaps she would see a ship wrecked.

She hoped in vain. Zeph had a poor opinion of the sea; he would have thought it no compliment to a respectable young girl to offer her a sight of that inscrutable nuisance. When they set out he turned his face firmly inland, conducting her to inspect Mr Hardwick's new silo. Sukey gazed with due respect at this rarity. It reminded her of the Tower of Babel, and she thought how dreadful it would be if Zeph suddenly began to speak French. After going up to the silo and tapping it with his stick, Zeph turned away. He did not break silence till they were on the Dannie road and about to cross on to the island—for here the creek was shrunk so small that a cart-track was carried across it on an earth embankment; then he looked back at an avenue of elm trees which stretched across the fields to Mr Hardwick's farmhouse. A large wain stood half-way up the avenue, looking as though no power could ever move it from the grass-grown ruts, and some white fowls were standing on it.

'Ah,' groaned Zeph, 'that's the last chaseway we shall see this day! And this is the last quickset hedge.'

He stroked the hedge with a loving and horny hand.

' Well, we can't look for comforts in the marsh, so 'tis idle to do so. God ordained marshes, but He didn't ordain 'em to be comfortable.'

He said no more till they were in sight of New Easter, when he mentioned the fact. Perhaps it was the obligation to speak no evil which had made Zeph a man of so few words. One would have to be cautious ; evil so soon slips out, and then, maybe, the thought would one day occur that the safest and simplest plan would be to speak not at all.

On Sunday mornings Zeph sat under the hay-rick reading his Bible, and when the dinner-bell rang he walked slowly up the path, singing Isaac Watts' Doxology to the tune *London Old*. The Nomans were Church people, and drove to Dannie church in the trap. Sunday dinner kept Sukey at home, but in the evening she was free to carry her prayer-book through the marsh. Whatever the weather, Dannie church was always cold and always fusty. The service was whisked through by a crumpled curate, whose sermons sounded as though he were so anxious to reach the end of his discourse that in his agitation he had forgotten the way out. Suddenly he would spy a gap in the hedge and leap out by it with a thanksgiving to God on his lips. It was not the style of preaching that Sukey was accustomed to : Mr James in London made the broad and the narrow paths as plain as if he were a steam-roller ; and sometimes she was tempted to envy Zeph the meetings of his Peculiar People, which took place in a parlour and finished with singing and seed cake.

But Zeph showed no more signs of being in a way to take her to meeting than he had shown of being in a way to take her to the sea, and in the end she found her way to the sea alone. As she walked along the wall she looked at the water in the creek ; that was going to the sea too, and swiftly, as if it had no fear of the waves. It ran with a chuckling voice. Its gliding haste bowed the sea-lavender and dandled a wisp of hay out of her sight. The path on the ridge of the wall was lost in long grass that pulled at her skirt. She stumbled perpetually, her ankles ached with being twisted, and then she saw a snake dart from before her feet and vanish into a bush. After this she walked with her eyes searching the ground, her ears pricked for a noise of hissing, so intent upon not setting foot on a snake that she forgot that she was in search of the sea, until she lost her footing completely and slipped half-way down the steep bank. Then, sitting in a nest of warm grass, she raised her eyes and saw something white, glittering white, that moved under the sky. A sail, the sail of a ship; and under it, and stretching out on either side as far as she could see, a strip of vehement blue.

A sensation of extraordinary buoyancy came over her, and it seemed to her that she also could spread sail and go laughing and fearless over that expanse of sapphire, sparkling and distantly resounding. A couple of butterflies settled on a leaf beside her, but they were not so blue as the sea; they were no more than two petals shed from that everlasting joy out there, beyond the saltings, beyond the earthy world. She sprang up and began to pick her way over the slabs of soft mud, wading through bushes of wild southernwood, setting her feet on thick cushions of samphire, jumping across the countless little channels by which the waters of the creek wound their way to the sea. But the mud became softer; if she stood for a moment hesitating where to place her next step she began to sink into it, and for every ditch she jumped there were two new ones to be negotiated, so that at last she was forced to own herself beaten: she could come no nearer to the sea, and for all the way she had come, twisting and turning, it looked as far away as ever, as joyous and as inaccessible. She turned inland and saw the grasses waving on the top of the sea-wall. Somewhere far off in the marsh a dog was barking, and then she heard a cock crow. Out here on the saltings she was in a secret place between two worlds, and putting her hand to her face to wipe off the sweat, she discovered that she smelled of this ambiguous territory—a smell of salt, of rich mud, of the bitter aromatic breath of the wild southernwood. She plunged her hands into a bush and snuffed into the palms. It was so exciting to discover herself thus perfumed—she, who till this day had never smelled of anything but yellow soap—that she suddenly found her teeth biting into her flesh, and that was a pleasure too, the bites were so small and even.

' I will come here every time I have an afternoon off,' she thought, as she walked home along the wall in the dusk. 'Why didn't I come before? Why didn't any one tell me? But now I have found it, and I would rather that I found it for myself.'

Yet, strange to say, Sukey did not go to the sea again. It was as if she had washed off its spell with the odour of the wild southernwood ; by the morrow her sensations of pleasure were irrecoverably lost, and it even seemed to her that she had run some terrible risk by going there, and that when she had stood on the saltings she had been made afraid.

The hot weather continued. The sky stretched its blue arch over the lapse of days, unvarying, as if it had forgotten clouds. Every morning Mr Noman would look upwards as he first stepped from the porch and say : ' Sky 's high.' Often, too, he cautioned Sukey not to waste the rain-water, for the iron tank being empty, there was no drinking water nearer than Ratten's Wick. Yet the heat was not oppressive, nor did the fields wear a look of drought, for every night the sea-mist refreshed them.

Sukey needed another cotton dress. She went to her tin box and took out the brown calico dress-length which had been given her as a prize. At the peculiar smell which arose from its folds she saw again the garden of the Warburton Memorial Female Orphanage, the cork grotto and the monkey-puzzle, and Mrs Seaborn sweeping over the sunburnt lawn. For a moment Mrs Seaborn seemed actually to approach her, when a flaw in the calico caught Sukey's eye. Would it come in the front breadth ? She measured and planned, shifting the heavy calico over her knee, till the striking clock called her downstairs. It was time to get supper ready, to call up the poultry for their evening feed, to fetch in the clothes that were drying on the line.

Supper was eaten and the table cleared before

she remembered that the striking clock had called
her from a consideration of something beyond
the flaw in the calico.   She remembered a com-
punction, but not, at first, its cause. She searched
back among her thoughts, trying to find the
turning which would lead her to her mislaid concern.   It was something left undone, something
to do with the orphanage.   Had she forgotten to
fish the blue-bag out of the tub, the last time she
worked in the laundry ?   It hung on a nail, and
underneath was a saucer to catch the drippings.

Suddenly the full recognition of that deflected
uneasiness flashed upon her, and she wondered
at herself.   How could she have forgotten Mrs
Seaborn so completely ?   Since she had arrived
at New Easter, she had scarcely given her a
thought.   She was overcome with shame for her
inconstancy and ingratitude—for had she not
vowed everlasting worship to that most beautiful, most worshipful of ladies ?—and to shame
succeeded fear. She feared that Mrs Seaborn
would come in, no longer dove-like and merciful,
but haughtily, with pale, affronted looks, to re-
proach her for her forgetfulness.   And again
she caught herself in fault, for how could Mrs
Seaborn be angry or show any mortal passion ?

But it was undeniable that she had forgotten
Mrs Seaborn, and presently she had to admit the

probability that she would forget her again, for now all memories of her former life were disused, and her past thoughts were strange to her, little more than the thoughts of some girl read of in a story. Perhaps it was through living upon an island.

Sukey was still persuaded that there was something very odd and exceptional about her life, though she, of course, was a very ordinary creature. In truth it was humdrum enough, and the cares and pleasures that filled her days were those common to any servant-girl on a small farm. Nor were the other inmates of the farm remarkable in any way that appeared to her. ' Bears,' so Prudence had called them. No doubt this was another of Prudence's misrepresentations, as baseless as her witness against the drake, and the bats, and the gun. Admittedly there was something a little bear-like about their stealthy, lumbering movements and the large gluttony of their table manners, but they were good bears, kindly disposed towards her, and showed their kind dispositions in the way that suited her best, seldom troubling her, except for another helping.

For some time Sukey credited Mr Noman with three sons : Reuben, Jem, and Eric ; but speaking of Eric to Reuben as ' your brother,' he stared, threw back his head like a horse, and exclaimed : ' Young Eric my brother ? That 's a good one, that is ! '

She was silent. Since Reuben chose to treat her to this jeering behaviour, she would inquire no further, nor justify herself in a very natural mistake. He prolonged his laughter till even to his own ears it must have rung false, for suddenly assuming a displeased air he added :

' He 's no relation of ours. Don't make that mistake again.'

After this she supposed that Eric was, like herself, inferior to the Nomans in social standing, though sufficiently above her to be addressed as Master Eric. Then, looking at him more curiously, she saw that he bore no mark of kinship to them, for they, all three, were large, swarthy men, and he was small and fair-skinned, with thick, wavy hair so thoroughly bleached that it was not possible to tell if its original tint inclined most to hay or honey. She was even further from intimacy with him than with the others, for he was scarcely ever within doors, coming in late for meals and sometimes not coming in for meals at all. Absent or present, he disturbed no one.

His youth, she supposed—for he seemed younger than herself—excused him from the degree of industry and responsibility which the farmer exacted from the rest of his household. Mr Noman was a strict and observant master, but if he asked Eric what he had been doing and Eric replied, 'Nothing,' the answer was given and accepted with a composure that showed it to be nothing out of the way.

One task, however, and that a task which should rightly have been Sukey's, was performed by him, for it was he who milked the cows. Sukey would gladly have learned how to milk, and Zeph had offered to teach her, shaking his head with disapproval when she explained that in London there had been no cows for her to learn on, but Mr Noman would not hear of it, saying that no one could strip the cows so thoroughly as Eric, and that upon this their yield depended. Sometimes she felt a little envious, hearing from the cowshed the sound of the milk striking against the sides of the pail, at first in spurts, then with a regular alternate drumming. Sometimes the sound of voices was added: Zeph, drawn to watch the peaceful sight, would try to teach Eric a hymn tune. Loudly and emphatically he sang the tune over, pausing between each line, and Eric would chime in after him with a low, tuneless humming where every note seemed to be struck on at random, the pitch rising and falling like the noise of the milk which streamed, now less, now more, between his steadily plying hands.

She was too shy to go into the cowshed, but if she could contrive to do so she would sneak into the yard on some pretext or other at milking-time, to get a handful of sticks from the woodshed maybe, to carry some sop to Mr Noman's ferrets, or to keep an eye on the cat. Especially did she like the evening milking, the cows returning from their day in the fields, walking slowly, conscious of their heavy udders, while the rays of the levelling sun brightened the russet of their coats, the rose-colour of their teats. She was soothed by their pleasure, and only regretted that she had no hand in it, for she would have liked to please everybody, and especially the cows.

Her first friendship at New Easter (for Zeph could not be quite counted as a friend, he was more like a waft of air mildly banging against her and smelling slightly of pigsties) was with a heifer. The heifer was red all over except for white socks on her hind-legs, white socks which gave her an air of gentility. Sukey thought of her as a young lady of quality, and when the beast waded in the pond Sukey would call out to her : ' Come back, Miss Tansy. You 'll dirty your feet.' Hearing the call, Tansy would move her ears forward as though she understood. Then very deliberately she would wade a step further in. Like a real young lady, she had a mind above white socks ; she was sure that they would always be renewed, however much people might scold, and she loved to wallow in the pond.

Tansy might well be a trifle arrogant, for she was very well born. She was sired by the most celebrated bull in Essex, Stingo the Third. The hair on her brow was as silky as a child's, and her coat glowed like a newly-husked chestnut. Mr Noman liked his stock to be red ; he said they looked more comfortable. Even the sheep were ruddled, and the hairy russet pigs had been brought all the way from Abbotsbury in Dorset to satisfy this whim of his. When the sow farrowed, Sukey felt rather ill at ease. She was abashed before such a large experience of maternity, and her embarrassment was complicated by Mr Noman having asked her if she knew how to cook a sucking-pig. She would have liked to condole with the sow, so rudely exploited by her young ones, but, knowing both so little and so much, she felt that her condolences would be open to a charge of hypocrisy, and also she was afraid of being overheard by the Nomans and laughed at.

From making friends with the beasts it seemed a natural step to make friends with Eric ; for not

only did he show himself to be, like her, most at
his ease in their company, but the preference
went further, it was almost affinity, as though he
belonged to some intermediate race between
human beings and animals. Intercoursing with
both, he was distinct from either, going his way
silent and untrammelled. The Nomans themselves seemed to take some such view of him.
They spoke of him always as ' Young Eric,' and
by their insistence upon his youthfulness seemed
to disassociate themselves from him. He was
like a pet lamb, grown too large for the house
but whom the household had forgotten to put
out of doors.

Though friendship with Eric might follow
upon friendship with beasts, it could not be so
easily prosecuted. Talk seemed to be too abrupt
a beginning : a question, a statement twitched
them apart again whom silence had drawn together. She must find some other way of ex-
pressing her kindness. But how ? She could
not scratch him behind the ear, or pull a tuft of
sweet grass to offer him. There appeared to be
nothing that she could do except to accustom
herself to feeling pleased in his company, and in
no other way, perhaps, could her timidity have
been so surely overcome ; for when the first
advances were made by him, they surprised

her no more than if they had been ripened in her own heart.

She was in the kitchen darning stockings when she felt something brush against her foot. It was a small striped apple. Looking up, she saw Eric standing in the doorway. She had heard no footsteps. She had no idea how long he had been there watching her, or if he were only just come ; that was Eric's way, she had long ago noticed that he was astonishingly light-footed. The Nomans clumped, she herself clattered, but Eric appeared noiselessly and noiselessly took himself off, as though he had the use of a pair of wings. Now, smiling, he took another apple from his pocket and rolled it across the floor towards her. With a laugh of triumph when it also came to her foot, he tossed a third apple into her lap.

'How pretty ! ' she said. 'Where do they come from ? There 's none of these grow in this garden surely ? '

'These apples never grew in our garden,' he answered.

'But where did you get them ? Has some one given them to you ? '

'Eat one,' said he, 'and if you like it, you shall have some more.'

Sukey bit into the reddest. It was surprisingly sour, almost like a crab-apple. She mastered the impulse to make a grimace, for she did not want to hurt his feelings.

' It *is* good.'

She took another cautious bite.

' Come with me and get some more.'

' But where do they grow ? '

' Out there,' he said, and waved his hand towards the marsh.

She had never seen him so animated. While he spoke, he kept tossing up his apples and catching them again, as dexterous and unconcerned as a juggler. Her curiosity was aroused. How could apples, even rather sour apples, grow in the marsh ? She looked at the clock.

' How long will it take to get there, Master Eric ? '

He tossed up the apples faster and faster ; they homed to his hand like tame birds.

' I thought you 'd want to come when you 'd tasted one.'

' But how long will it take ? '

' It 's a mile there and a mile back. Can you walk two miles ? '

' I 'll come,' she said. ' After all, I can darn as well out of doors as in.'

Leaving the farm, they walked northward into the centre of the island. The landscape lay

before them as clear as a chart : fields scantly enclosed, a distant rickyard, a few dwarfed thorn-
trees, a couple of willows broken to bridge the
drain that serpentined hither and thither—an un-
promising landscape in which to look for apples.
Carrying the darning-basket, Sukey walked behind
her guide.   He had fallen silent again, but his air
of animation persisted.   He cleared the drain
with a running jump, and once, when he turned
to point at a heron, she saw that a smile of satisfied achievement still played about his lips.

He stopped suddenly before a patch of
stinging-nettles and brambles.

' Look ! ' said he, and pointed to it.

For a moment she wondered if there was a
kind of wild apple that grew upon brambles, then
she saw some scattered bricks.   The turf was
swallowing them up, the brambles trailed among
and over them.

She looked to him for an explanation.

' There was a house here once,' he said.
' This is where the chimney stood.'

' But why did it fall down ?   What became of
the people ? '

' I don't know.   Perhaps the birds picked out
their eyes.'

Sukey shuddered and looked reproachfully
about her. The solitude of the landscape weighed

upon her vision ; she felt afraid of the marsh.
Turning once more to Eric, she found he was
gone.   Her fears blazed up like a straw fire ; she
opened her lips to call to her companion, but no
sound came from them, and when at last she
found voice, her cry, wavering over the silent
marsh, increased her panic.   It sounded all un-
familiar, the very voice of fear.

'Oh, where are you ? '

'Here ! '

'But where ?   I can't see you.'

'Here—in the orchard.'

The words came from beyond a straggling
belt of thorn-trees.   She ran towards them and
scrambled through their defences.   He stood
before her, seemingly unconscious of her disturbance.

'Now you can pick all the apples you want.'

The thorns had once hedged in a little orchard.
Here were cankered apple-trees, plum-trees
weighed down with fruit small and thickly-
bloomed as grapes, cherries, sloes and bullaces,
and in the midst of these, like a queen, a pear-
tree with its straight round stem.   The fruit lay
scattered in the long grass—small sour apples,
insipid pears fallen unripe from the tree, sloes
tasting of iron ; only the plums had kept a curious watery sweetness.   For a time they strayed

in silence, amusing themselves with the fruit, biting once and throwing away ; then they sat down under the pear-tree. Sukey spread out the contents of the darning-basket and wondered at her fears : this was a peaceful place in which to play at keeping house.

The shadows wandered over their faces, and a soft wind ruffled Eric's hair, blowing the outer locks aside. He lay along the grass, his gaze fixed and unspeculative. Looking sideways from her darning, she could scrutinize him at her leisure without being rude. She saw how the sun striking between the leaves outlined his nose with a little golden halo. She saw how closely freckled was the fine skin below his eyes ; she measured the low brow and the short upper lip ; she explored the curious pattern of his ear. Black as a crow herself, and deploring her blackness—for were not black looks akin to wickedness ?—she admired almost with reverence his fair, unemphatic beauty. She was astonished at the fineness of his hair, whose true colour, as the wind rifted it, she discovered to be the pale greenish gold of honey. God, whose hand had polished every glistening thread, might number those hairs, but who else could ? For the first time in her life, she apprehended the beauty of the human make : the beauty, not of fine eyes or a white hand, but of each hair distinct and wonderful, of the delicate varied grain of the skin. Thus admiring him, she no longer despised herself, and seeing her hands at their work, she forgot to think of them as red and coarsened with labour, observing only how deft they were in movement, how fit in their proportions.

The sound of the Dannie church clock told her at last that it was time to return home. Before leaving the orchard she glanced back in farewell. The lengthened shadows gave it a secret look. She wondered if she or Eric would be asked where they had spent the afternoon, and she hoped not. Mr Noman would not mind, he often told her that she should go out more while the fine weather lasted, but Prudence Gulland was now an open visitor to New Easter, her former disgrace, whatever it was, having been patched over, and Sukey dreaded what Prudence might say. She would joke and ask nudging questions, and then, perhaps, Eric would be rebuffed, and retreat into his lair of silence. She held him but by one slight thread, an afternoon spent pleasantly together; one wince back on his part and he would be lost to her. She did not want to lose him now; if she lost him, she would feel friendless, though she had not felt friendless before. But no one asked questions, and by bedtime the excursion seemed as securely private as an excursion of the mind. Eric was silent and aloof as ever; if their eyes met, his glance acknowledged no share of recollection. Had she gone to the orchard alone and but imagined him beside her, he could not have been more unconcerned. This did not grieve her, or offend her, for it seemed natural that it should be so. In silence they had been drawn to each other, had greeted each other in a kind of obscurity; silence and obscurity were as much a part of their pleasure as its colour is part of a flower. She was content to have it thus; indeed, she could not imagine how it should be otherwise.

She could see that Eric disliked Prudence as much as she did. Prudence seemed able to do what no one else could do—to make him feel uncomfortable; in her presence he was awkward and childish, even his bodily grace deserting him. He watched her like an animal that remembers a kicking, and whenever she spoke to Sukey he frowned. But Prudence did not often speak to Sukey. She hoped to marry Reuben, and thought that by treating the farm-servant as beneath her notice she could persuade Mr Noman to forget that she had been in the same position herself. Sukey did not mind how rude Prudence might be to her—in fact, the ruder she was the better, for then there was less risk of being drawn into conversation with her, Prudence's conversation having always the effect of renewing that first feeling of uneasiness, of being exposed to some lurking danger ; but she wished that she would not come so often to New Easter, disturbing Eric and driving him out to wander in the marsh alone. She would have liked to wander with him, but how could she ? For all his silence, his thistledown air of diffidence, she knew certainly that it must depend on his election, not hers, whether she might go too.

At last the invitation came. He spoke doubtfully, almost as though their first excursion had never taken place.

' Where shall we go ? ' she said. ' To the orchard ? '

His face lit up as though her words had unlocked some answer in his mind.

' Yes, to the orchard.'

The former understanding was suddenly reestablished, and they followed the path through the marsh as if they had walked along it together many times. They passed the patch of brambles and the ruined hearth, and Eric led the way through the gap in the hedge. As Sukey stepped through after him, he turned to her ; the earnestness of his expression took her aback.

'Don't be frightened,' he said. 'Don't be frightened, Sukey.'

He caught hold of her hand and fondled it, putting it inside his coat as though it were something to be sheltered, a bird, perhaps, that had fallen out of its nest on a morning when the spring wind blew cold. She stared at him in bewilderment. She understood nothing of what was happening ; she only understood his extreme anxiety to comfort, to reassure her. He took her in his arms and held her to him, patting her shoulder and kissing her as though he were comforting a child. She had almost forgotten how to think when the memory of the time before, and of how she had been afraid of the bramble-patch, flashed back on her.

'But, Eric, I am not frightened now.'

'No, not now, not now.'

He held her more closely ; his kisses settled upon her cheek like a flight of doves. Suddenly he released her and stood back, looking at her with a face of shining triumph.

'You're not frightened now, Sukey, are you?'

She shook her head. She did not know what to do, what to say, but seeing him smile she smiled back at him.

'Sukey, how pretty you are! Your head is so smooth and black, it is like a sloe.'

Gravely taking her hand, he led her to the pear-tree and settled her upon the grass ; then, leaning against the tree, he looked down on her with a sheltering glance. She felt the tears come into her eyes—never could she have dreamed that any one should be so kind to her. In all her life no one had kissed her so, nor spoken to her so tenderly. She took hold of his hand and leaned her cheek against it.

'Kind !' she said. 'Kind !'

She had forgotten everything except this new pleasure of being cherished. With a sigh she drew him to sit down beside her, and offered her mouth to be kissed. Above his face, shadowy and strange with proximity, and the near bright glitter of his eyes, she saw the pattern of oval leaves ; like a sweet net it seemed to descend on her and close her in.

So this was love :—she wished that she were not so ignorant about it. This love was so sweet a thing that it seemed almost an ingratitude never to have thought about it, never to have looked forward to its coming. If she had known, she would have prepared herself, she would have made her heart into a nest for it, but here she was, a girl who scarcely knew how to kiss, unpractised in endearments save those which she had given to Tansy the heifer, or to the funny little pigs, accepting love without any of the repaying graces which are love's due. Eric must find her stupid and awkward, though he did not seem to mind, and in her thoughts she often apologised to him for lacking thus, and explained that it was not really her fault. Love had not been stressed at the orphanage. God could love—love so greatly that He had once become a man who died for sinners because He loved them so much. But that was long ago, and now His love was less haphazard, less headlong. 'God will not love you,' Miss Pocock used to say to the smaller orphans when they quarrelled in the playground. 'Those whom the Lord loveth He chasteneth,' said Mr James, the clergyman. He spoke of God's love made manifest in this chastening fashion, telling of good negroes beaten in swamps, of the awakening sick-bed pangs of sinners that God had taken a fancy to, and of the sufferings of the French Protestants ; and on Sunday evenings in Advent, when the prowling darkness outside had closed in upon the window with the Good Shepherd in it and made it all quite black, he would preach about the birth of Christ, and of His Second Coming. That would be a very different affair. Once in his fervour Mr James blew out the pulpit candle. Some one giggled. 'It would be well for sinners,' said he, after the verger had lit the candle again, 'if God's wrath could blow out their souls as I have blown out this candle. But we are candles that can never be blown out, or burn away, and many must burn in hell for ever.'

This was a terrible God to love ; even to be loved by Him had its terrors. As for earthly love, that was nothing compared to His, so very properly the orphanage authorities never mentioned it. Sukey, however, had picked up a few stray notions here and there, for sometimes the elder girls would get together and whisper, saying how nice it would be to be loved by a young man. Poor Milly Fisher with the club foot was so sure of this that notwithstanding her lameness she managed to creep out one evening and stay away all night. When she returned she had no chance of telling the others if her faith was justified, for she was immediately haled before Miss Pocock and no one saw her again until she was expelled in front of everybody and taken mute away by a large angry man whom some declared to be her uncle and others a warder from prison.

After this the elder girls whispered more than ever, but now they whispered of the dreadful things which follow upon love with a young man. Something might happen and then you died. ' It 's babies you die of,' said Annie

Parker. Sukey thought this very likely; she well remembered her mother holding on to the mangle, crying with pain and saying among her tears that she would certainly die of her next, as indeed in the end she had done. But Jane Dyson shook her head and declared that it was something worse than babies.

Sukey did not now suppose that as a result of love she would die. It was vivifying to be loved by Eric; his earthly love did not frighten her as that heavenly love might have done. But she thought it very likely that she would have a baby, and sometimes she was almost sure that she could feel a slight pain inside which must be the baby beginning. Sukey had good principles; she knew that it is wrong to have a baby unless you are married. She decided that she must talk seriously to Eric.

Unfortunately this was more easily decided than done. Eric was both kind and dear; he kissed her with gentle, rapid kisses like the fluttering of a bird's wing, and when they walked together to the orchard he held back the brambles lest they should scratch her, and took great care that she should not set her feet in a cow-pat; but for all his tenderness he seemed resolved to show his mastery over her, and this by never allowing her to be serious. Try as she would to be grave,

and to make him so by example, he was never
at a loss for some trick by which to surprise her
into gaiety. Like a pet animal that wants a game
and by treating each rebuff as an inspired sally
of playfulness at last cajoles its master into playing in good earnest, he laughed at her serious
face and made her laugh by his mimicry of it
until he had coaxed her into a frolicking spirit
that was ready to run races with his own. And
then, when she had yielded, he looked at her
with a merry, artless triumph, like one sure of
his power, so sure that he need never give it a
thought nor consciously exert it.

In the light of such a countenance, it was not
possible for her to think that she did wrong ; it
could never be wrong for her to love him or to
admit his love ; but still it was not right to have
a baby without a wedding first. Babies are not
as harmless as love ; they require justification,
since while love only makes two people happy, a
baby may grow up and make any number of
people miserable. Besides justification, they
also require long clothes and short clothes and
little woollen socks—and how is an unmarried
baby going to find these ?

Sukey believed that children born out of wedlock must either die or be taken to the Foundling
Hospital, where they grow up with a numbered

ticket round their necks and are whipped if they cry. She could not bear it if such things were to happen to her child, and still less to a child that would be Eric's too, a creature that would really and truly need all the cherishing and solicitude that she felt for her lover but was never quite able to bestow, she herself being so diffident and he so masteringly and serenely gay. She made up her mind that for once she must compel him to take life seriously. By herself she knew that she was not able to do this thing, so she made a plan for securing the assistance of a very important ally—no other, as the collect recommends, than God; and when next they went for a walk together, she chose the way along the track that led inland to Dannie.

The Dannie churchyard was very quiet and very old. It was so old that the dead who lay there had raised the level of the ground by six or seven feet, and in the flatness of the marsh this elevation was something considerable. Eric and Sukey climbed the holy hill and sat down under the shade of an ilex-tree. Immediately in front of them was a tombstone with the inscription : *Here lies Thomas Purr, aged one year and two months.*

'He must have died when he was a kitten,' said Eric.

When he looked at Sukey, she was crying.

He threw the daisy-chain he was making over her head and kissed her, but she turned away her face and continued to cry. He asked her what was the matter, but she could not answer for her tears. Though he was quiet and gentle, as she had hoped the churchyard would make him, she knew now that she could never ask him to marry her, for she loved him so much that she was abashed to ask for anything. And so her baby would be born out of wedlock and must either die or go to the Foundling Hospital and have a ticket with a number on it instead of a name.

With a feeling of despair she saw that Eric had risen to his feet and was looking at her as though he would presently persuade her to play. And then she must yield, she must put away her tears and go on playing, for he loved her, and his light-hearted love was not to be denied.

'Listen, Sukey, I'll tell you what we'll do. We'll go into church and be married. We can easily climb in through a window.'

She began to laugh, for her tenderness towards him was like a wild thing tickling her bosom.

'O my darling,' she exclaimed, 'what a silly you are! For we can't be married without a clergyman.'

His face fell. She took his hand and explained

how many things are needed for a marriage—a ring, a clergyman, and the calling of the banns.

'But if you want me to marry you, I will marry you with all my heart, and love you all my life long, my dearest, as I love you now. And on the way home we will be very sensible, and talk about what we must do to get married.'

But on the way home they laughed and ran races, for the wind was getting up, blowing in moist from the sea, and it bunted against them like a friendly dog that wants to play. The marsh darkened about them; behind them the ilex-trees of the Dannie churchyard were rising and falling and roaring like a sombre steadfast wave; layers of thin grey cloud were hurrying over the sky, covering it from east to west, weaving a swift-coming darkness. The long taciturn autumn that had endured into the last week of November was suddenly at an end, and now, as through a breach in the sea-wall, in the space of a couple of hours the winter had come flooding in over the marsh. With every gust of wind, with every increment of darkness, a nameless ecstasy and excitement seemed to be rising up all around. Even the water in the drains and land-locked pools, which ever since she had been in the marsh Sukey had seen mutely and sullenly swelling and diminishing, was now come to life, was moving against the banks with curt slapping sounds and ruffling up its surface against the wind.

A wisp of straw blew past them like a witch on a broomstick, and the crouched thorns clapped their skeleton hands. Sukey ran faster and faster; her skirts blew out and she thought that she could mount on the wind. She was not glad because winter was upon them; whistling grasses and rattling thorn and the far-off ilex-wave tumbling and bellowing—none of these had any more reason than she to be rejoicing in the winter wind, and yet she felt everywhere rising up and enveloping her a raving welcome in which she too must join, though it were against her will, just as when people are watching a burning house, though each one individually may be sorry or appalled, yet the common spirit is on the fire's side, and shouts and triumphs with each volley of flame.

In the porch she stopped to tidy her hair and scrape the mud off her boots. She wished that she could tidy her face too—she was afraid the Nomans would notice how wild she looked. Her wind-blown cheeks stung as she slipped into the hot bright kitchen, and catching sight of herself in the speckled mirror, she blushed redder still at the reflection of this coloured, quick-breathing creature with shining eyes, so unlike the Sukey that they knew.

But the Nomans had other fish to fry, as soon appeared, for hearing her come in, Prudence Gulland cried out :

' Reuben 's got a piece of news for you, Suke. You ask him ! '

Sukey looked politely at Reuben, who was silent. Prudence nudged him.

' Go on, Reuben ! Don't be bashful.'

After some more nudging, Reuben said :

' I 'm a-going to have her.'

Now it was his turn to nudge Prudence, who drew herself up and told him sharply to keep his hands to himself. But her satisfaction over-flowed her dignity, and she soon forgot about Reuben's hands as she informed Sukey that she and Reuben were to be married at the new year, and that Mr Noman was going to give them a wardrobe with a glass in it, and that Mrs Gulland had promised a marble-topped washstand and a feather bed, and that the engagement ring on her finger had cost one pound ten and was real gold and real stones, and that she had decided on a wedding-dress already—fawn colour with pink trimmings and a fur boa.

' And I shall be mistress of New Easter,' she concluded. ' And you 'll take your orders from me, and you 'll have to run round quick, I can tell you, so now you know what to look out for. Cheer up, Suke ! I dare say you 'll get a boy in time—they do say one wedding brings another— so don't stand there looking so wrought-up, but come and wish me joy.'

Sukey wished joy to Prudence as she was requested, and also to Reuben, whose amorous breathing seemed to fill the whole kitchen. She glanced at Mr Noman, wondering what she ought to wish him ; she could see that joy would not be quite the right wish, but to wish him strength to endure and forbearance in his affliction would be impertinent, so she asked him if she should cook anything extra for supper.

' No, not to-night,' Prudence answered for him. ' But I 'm stopping here for the night and to-morrow we 'll have a blow-out and eat that pecking cockerel. He 's in the pen now, being fasted, and to-morrow you 'll have to kill him. Crrrwk ! '

Prudence imitated the cockerel's death-rattle. She knew how greatly Sukey disliked killing poultry.

Meanwhile it had not occurred to Sukey to compare her lot with Prudence's. She, too, this afternoon had been asked in marriage, but between Eric and herself, Prudence and Reuben, there did not seem to be anything in common. She was as far from despising the other two for their exuberant mating as from envying them; she heard the news, accepted it, wished them their joy of it—but it was all something irrelevant that could cast neither light nor shadow on her own secret joy. She looked round for Eric. He was sitting at the other end of the kitchen, mending a wicker basket. He had taken no part in the conversation, and no one had expected him to do so. To all appearances he was perfectly unconcerned; he might have been unaware of what they were all talking about. But when the time for good-nights came and Sukey was leaving the room, he suddenly caught hold of her left hand and gave the ring finger a little nip. No one saw, and in a moment he had turned away; but long after the candle was blown out, and even after Prudence, who was sharing the better half of her bed, had left off glorying, Sukey lay with that finger against her lips, fancying that she could yet feel a tingle there.

She was awakened by the noise of Prudence yawning and groaning. The rain was splashing out of the gutters, and the wind rattled the doors and window-frames. Then a cock crew on a whooping and melancholy note.

'Devil take the rain!' lamented Prudence.

She stretched, and her hand struck against Sukey's shoulder. ' Hullo ! ' she said. ' Who are you ? ' She caught hold of Sukey's plait and gave it a tweak. 'Lawks ! You 're Suke. And I 'm to be married to Reuben at the new year. Blest if I hadn't forgotten all about it. Wake up, Suke ! Light a candle and see what time it is.'

There was still half an hour before Sukey need get up, but there was to be no more rest for her that morning, for now that Prudence had remembered her affianced estate she was as flown with satisfaction and excitement as she had been overnight. She was also, since they were alone, a good deal more confidential. Sukey listened without comment to Prudence's views on the character of the man whom she proposed to marry.

' He 's a boy, I can tell you. Carries on like a gentleman almost. If his Dad knew as much about his goings-on as I do, he wouldn't be best pleased, and that 's a fact. But he 's only got himself to blame for bringing 'em up so strict, never a bit of larking allowed from one year's end to another. Jem 's just such another. There 's a girl in Shoebury as can tell you all about Jem. And yet I dunno. They 're all the same, men are, however you bring 'em up. I daresay the old man himself ain't as prim as he lets on to be. But Reuben 'll have to change his manners once I 've got a firm hold on him. If he tries it on with me, he 'll get a surprise or two, for I won't have my husband making a fool of me, and that 's flat. What are you looking so shocked about? First you 've heard about it, I suppose.'

'It 's no business of mine what Reuben and Jem do.'

'No, I should hope it ain't no business of yours what Reuben and Jem do. Nor it won't be no business either, and don't you forget it, or you 'll be out of here like a cat with a half-brick heaved after it, or my name won't be Prudence Noman.'

'Don't be cross, Prudence. I only meant I hadn't noticed anything.'

'Good gracious, any one would think the girl went about with her head in a sack! But there, don't look as if I was going to eat you. I don't mean you any harm. But you are a caution. It beats me how any London girl can be so harmless. A kitten with its eyes shut knows more than you do. Strikes me, Suke, it 's high time I came to New Easter to look after you. I says to Mother only two nights ago, I says : " There 's that girl alone at New Easter, no more able to look out for herself than the babe unborn ; a fair

scandal I calls it. However could that Mrs Seaborn have sent her there? Does she think," I
says, " as Suke Bond is as knowing as she is?"
And Mother, she says: " 'Tisn't only men,
Prudence, it 's bulls, roaming all over the marsh
as she does by herself. However she can do it
passes my intellect." And you was out again last
night, wasn't you? Wherever had you been,
coming back like that after dark?'

' To Dannie.'

' To Dannie? What did you do there?'

' Sat in the churchyard.'

' Sat in the churchyard? Sat in that churchyard alone? You might have seen a ghost and
gone raving mad.'

Sukey was silent.

' Were you alone?'

' No. Eric was with me.'

' Eric! Do you mean to tell me that you were
out in the marsh with *him*? Well, all I can say
is, don't you ever do such a thing again, or
maybe you 'll be sorry for it.'

' Why?'

' Because he ain't to be trusted.'

Sukey got out of bed and began to dress. She
was thankful that Prudence's new dignity would
oblige her to lie a-bed till breakfast-time. The
tingle was quite gone from her ring finger now;

Prudence's words had had their accustomed effect and she felt angry and miserable. What did it mean, that Eric was not to be trusted? Why should she ever be sorry for going out alone with him in the marsh? Was the marsh so cruel, so wicked, that it might make him wicked and cruel too? Did it hate lovers so much, the marsh that had lost the sea, that it could in some way bring down their love to ruin? She remembered the afternoon on the saltings: something had frightened her then, though what it had been that frightened her she could not say. She had slipped on a bank of silver mud; for a moment she had not been able to lift her feet from that soft heavy grip, and looking down into the channel she had seen a small crab sidle away. Perhaps it was that which had been so frightening. And then there was the time when she had first seen the bricks lying under the bramble-patch, when Eric had spoken of the people who had once sat by that hearth, and had said that the birds had picked out their eyes. Were they lovers, and had the marsh envied them their happiness, their fireside safety? But then Eric had taken pity on her fear; in the midst of the lonely marsh he had wrapped her round with the security of being loved. Eric was kind, Eric loved her; only yesterday he had wanted to

marry her, had suggested—the darling silly!—
that they should climb in at the church window
to get married. Why should she mind what
Prudence said? She knew Eric a great deal
better than Prudence did. But for all that the
words came back to her: *He's not to be trusted.*
If only I could see him! she thought. If only he
would come in now, I should be at peace again!
I have only to look at him to know that it is all
right.

Eric was milking the cows, but as ill luck
would have it, Prudence came down just before
he carried in the milk-pails. He set them down
without a word and went out again.

'I'll do the milk!' Prudence suddenly exclaimed.

She lifted the pail and began to pour the milk
into the shallow bowls. In her haste to show off
before Sukey she was clumsy; she knocked the
edge of the pail against the table and the milk
slopped out.

'Drat it, why should I break my back?
Reuben!'

She went to the door and called into the rainy
dusk.

'Reuben! Come in here. I want you.'

Reuben appeared at the doorway, grinning.

'Come and give me a hand with these pails.'

'What about my boots?' he inquired.

' Never mind your boots. The floor 's got to be sluiced anyhow. Heave up this pail for me, there 's a dear.'

' Going to be a farmer's wife and can't heave up a milk-pail. What else do you want doing for you ? Like me to heave up your back hair for you next, I suppose.'

Sukey felt that there was no place for her in the dairy, so full of Prudence and Reuben bandying kisses and repartees ; even the ceiling was invaded with their interlacing shadows. She sneaked away to the back-kitchen (but there was no need to sneak ; if she had gone out on her head, she told herself, they would not have noticed her going, for they had each other to attend to) and began to fry bacon and eggs. The wind blew in under the door and chilled her feet, while her face was scorched with the heat rising up from the spluttering fat. She was alone, but there was no chance that Eric would come in now ; she would not see him till breakfast. And then it would all be as usual ; he would sit there like one in a dream, like one in another world, vaguely smiling or staring at the roses on the milk-jug ; if by chance their eyes met, he would meet her glance without a sign of recognition or remembrance. And yet this was her lover, and yesterday they had spoken of marriage.

Now Prudence's words rang out with a new meaning : *He 's not to be trusted*. And that was true. How was it possible to trust in one so careless, so elusive—a lover who for an hour was near and close and the hour after was more strange to her than any stranger, a lover who seemed able to forget her words and kisses as utterly as though they were a dream lost in awakening ? How could she trust him ? She might as well try to lean on a rainbow.

Breakfast was everything that she had expected it to be and worse, for in the middle of the meal the lamp went out. Mr Noman was in a bad temper ; he scolded her for carelessness, and Prudence made a joke about foolish virgins. Reuben and Jem broke into loud guffaws, and Eric, who had not appeared to be paying the least attention to what was going on, suddenly laughed too. Mr Noman struck his fist on the table.

' I will have no jeering at Bible matters in my house, and I tell you so once for all. If you can't talk decently, don't talk at all.'

After that they sat in silence, listening to the wind and the rain, till Mr Noman got up to go out. At the door he paused and looked at Sukey.

' Don't forget the cockerel,' he said.

It was as well that he spoke, for in the confused distress and flurry of her mind the fact that she must kill the cockerel had clean escaped her. Now this thought seemed to clinch all the miseries of this miserable morning. Prudence, whom she hated, was going to marry Reuben, was coming to live at New Easter—to bear rule over her, to take away her peaceful stewardship in kitchen and dairy, to harry her with commands, and with confidences far more repulsive than any commands could be, to frighten her from her happiness in being loved, to spy on her, to entrap her in fears and doubts as in a dirty cobweb, to close her up in a pit of mental servitude where Eric would never come to her again ; and because of this she must kill the cockerel for the betrothal feast.   She put up her hands to the back of her neck and pressed the fingers into the flesh, and thrust with her neck against the pressure like an animal rearing against the yoke.   She must kill the cockerel, whether she would or no, for in this dark house, where everything had with the coming of winter suddenly become harsh and treacherous, there was no one to stand up for her, there was no one to take her part.

She became aware that Prudence was looking at her, and that on Prudence's face there was a leer of malevolence and contempt.

' I shall kill the cockerel now,' she said.

' How are you going to do it ? '

' With the chopper.'

' No, that you won't ! '

Prudence jumped up and came over to her.

' You 're to stick it, do you hear ? That bird 's
for my eating, and I 'm the one to say how it 's to
be killed. And I say it 's to be stuck and let
bleed properly, because that way it 'll eat more
refined.'

As Prudence said these last words she glared
down into Sukey's face as though it were Sukey
that she wanted to eat most. Her eyes were
rather bloodshot, and noticing this Sukey was
filled with sudden scorn and feared her no longer.

' Just as you please.'

She walked out of the kitchen, holding herself
very erect, and slammed the door behind her.
In the back-kitchen she took up the slender knife
which she was to jab down the cockerel's gullet,
and went out across the yard to the cart-shed,
walking bareheaded under the rain, still in a sort
of trance of defiance.

The cockerel had been shut up in a wicker pen
at the back of the cart-shed. There was a leak
in the roof just above him, and he was drenched
with rain, his feathers darkened and plastered together, his comb and wattles discoloured with
long cold. All his fierceness was drowned out
of him ; he made no struggle as Sukey lifted him

out of the pen, but crouched under her arm, shivering and croaking sadly to himself. At the end of his long dangling legs his claws feebly clenched and unclenched the air.

'He won't notice much,' she said, and carried the bird towards the block. 'I should think he'd be glad to die.'

It seemed to her that she had no feelings except scorn, and that she despised the cockerel for his lack of spirit. She glanced down at the bird, and he looked back at her with his flat, unreal eye. Suddenly she knew that she could not and would not slaughter this creature, so disconsolate and unlovable.

'I won't!' she exclaimed. 'Why should I have to? I won't! They can kill their own bird if they want it.'

She put it down in the middle of the yard. It stood at her feet, motionless and drooping.

'Shoo! Shoo! Get along with you, you silly creature! Shoo! Oh, for Heaven's sake, shoo!'

The cockerel did not stir.

It seemed to her somehow essential that the bird should justify her revolt by making some effort to save itself, and she began to shake her wet skirts at it. Just then Eric came into the yard. He showed no surprise to see her standing there bareheaded in the driving rain, her indoor clothes soaked and clinging about her, and the cockerel motionless at her feet. He looked at her, smiled with casual friendliness, and went on towards the house.

'Stop!' she cried. 'Come here!'

He turned and came towards her, stepping lightly over the sodden earth, seeming to move as unconcernedly, as purposelessly, as easily as a feather blown on the wind. Under the shadow of an old slouch hat his eyes were as bright as gems. The wind howled, the air was murky and filled with the sounds of tempest, a vapour of rain blotted out all colour, all form, all reality; everything was submerged in a twilight of desolation, as though New Easter amid the marshes crouched at the bottom of the sea and was darkened and buffeted by the tramplings of a storm which raged far overhead.

But Eric, moving lightly towards her, his face sleeked with rain, his eyes small and bright under the shadow of his hat, did not seem to mind, did not seem to notice. He was in his own world, mysterious and apart as ever, and from this world of his own, through the windows of his bright eyes, he looked out at her, regarding her with extraordinary secret excitement, an excitement she could not share, could not understand.

Never before had he seemed to her so beautiful, never so enthralling ; never before had she seen him so plainly nor with such entire spellbound attention.   It was as though his aloofness were a sleep, withholding her from him, yet allowing her to gaze on him with undivided mind, and for a long moment she forgot everything—her distress, her doubts, her need of him, her purpose in calling him towards her—just to look at him.

But now he was at her side, his cold hand had taken hold of her chin—he was going to kiss her. His gaze would plunge unswerving into hers and drown her in darkness.   She twisted herself back, blinking, holding open her eyes with an effort.

'Take care ! You 'll frighten it. The cockerel.'

He picked up the bird and began to caress it, blowing softly into the hackle of its neck.

' What 's the matter, Sukey ?   What do you want ? '

What she wanted to say was :

' Save me !   You must save me, for I am in despair and only you can rescue me.   I am alone, I am in love, I am terrified out of my wits. Everything is in a conspiracy against me, everything menaces me, everything is new and unknown and terrifying, for love has changed it, and changed me too, so that I can do nothing to save myself, I can only whirl to and fro among my fears. Oh, save me, you ought to save me, for I am yours, I have given myself to you, I am not my own any longer. And yet I don't feel as though you had got me. I am like a ghost, I don't know myself any longer. I am like a dream. The sight of my own hand is enough to startle me, it seems strange and not mine. I am like *your* dream, and you may wake up and forget me, and I shall never be able to find my way to you any more. And you are like *my* dream. For after all I know nothing about you, sometimes I feel as though I had never set eyes on you before. Oh, make yourself real to me! Do something, say something, be like a real person. Don't just kiss me and wander away again. I am not just something you kiss. I am Sukey Bond, and you have asked me to marry you. I am Sukey Bond, and I am going to bear your child. I am Sukey Bond, and I love you. Give me something real to love, be kind to me, be real to me, show me that you understand, take away my fears! For you can do it so easily. A word would do it—I think even if you were to sneeze that would do it. But you must do it now. Yes, now, now, at this very moment! For if you drift away again, if you hide yourself from me in a kiss and are gone without understanding what's the matter with me, if you won't understand what I don't understand myself, I shall die. I cannot bear to be left alone with my love for you any longer. Show yourself, be real to me, let me trust you, come alive and take this love that I cannot give to you properly unless you open yourself to it and take it in ! '

So she would have spoken, while her eyes were fixed upon his lips and on the passage of his breath, softly wandering through the bird's plumage. When she spoke it was to say, coldly and challengingly :

' That bird 's got to be killed. And I don't see why you shouldn't do it for me. Reuben lifts the milk-pails for Prudence, so I think you might kill that cockerel for me.'

He looked at her, slightly frowning.

' Don't look so cross, Sukey. I 'll kiss you if you like.'

' Here 's the knife,' she said, and held it out to him with downcast eyes. Her hand trembled. The wind was blowing so violently that the ground seemed to be rocking under her feet.

Eric put down the cockerel and turned away.

The wind blew harder. The corner of a piece of tarpaulin on one of the ricks had come unfastened and threshed up and down with a banging noise. Oh, he was not to be trusted! He did not love her, he did not care what became of her, he would always desert her in her need. But she loved him, he was hers, she had a claim on him, to trust him was only her due. He must pay her her due ; if she did not enforce it now, she might lose him for ever. She snatched up the cockerel, ran after Eric, thrust the bird into his arms.

' You must ! ' she exclaimed. ' You must ! I love you. You must help me.'

He did not answer, and she began to haul him towards the chopping-block. She seemed to be struggling with a dream, and because he came passively, yielding himself to her hands, it increased her desperation ; it was as though by his very passiveness he had eluded her will far more completely than he could have done by any resistance. Now she put the knife into his hand, but he held it loosely, and though when she had closed his fingers upon it they remained as she had arranged them, he did not seem to have the least idea what it was that he must do. The cockerel began to struggle. It freed one wing from under Eric's arm and beat the air. Eric dropped the knife and tried to quiet it, tickling its breast, making condoling noises to it, while it pecked at his hand. So he had striven to soothe her, once, long ago, in the orchard.

Suddenly all her tumult of feeling fell away from her, and in the midst of the racing wind she stood in an utter and glassy calm. Yes, that was how it was. He had said: 'Don't be frightened. Don't be frightened, Sukey,' and taking her hand he had fondled it as if it were a bird. He was sorry for birds. He loved all helpless things, all wild things, all harmless and thoughtless things, for he himself was wild and harmless, thoughtless and helpless. He was sorry for the bird, he understood its distress. *Her* distress he could not understand. It passed by him like the wind —violent, alien, incomprehensible. Her anger was a flame that would not take upon him. And now, when perhaps she had lost him for ever, he would not understand her despair.

'O my dear,' she said, 'forgive me! Poor Eric, of course you couldn't kill it!'

And taking the cockerel from his arms she looked at it through tears, and said:

'Poor bird!'

For though it had pecked her time and time again, and though it had been the cause of all this turmoil, and though arbitrary death was the end of all cockerels, she was grieved for it and felt that it was a shame that it must be killed for Prudence's vindictive eating. At any rate, she thought, you shan't suffer more than you need. And, taking up the chopper, she aimed, and struck.

The blow was true. The blood leapt out in an arch of scarlet on the grey curtain of rain. And with a loud cry Eric had fallen to the ground and lay there, his hand clutching the bloodied earth, his face convulsed, his breath snoring and sobbing.

She fell on her knees beside him. She raised his head on her lap. She began to search for the wound, for it seemed to her that somehow she must have struck him in striking at the cockerel. But there was no wound, no blood except the blood smeared on his hand. Yet he groaned and quivered like something done to death. She called out wildly for help, but the wind tore the sounds from her mouth and scattered them. No one would hear her, however she called. She must leave him there and run to fetch them. But as she rose to her feet, his hand, straying over the bloodied earth, caught hold of her skirt and fastened upon it, and once more she cast herself down beside him and tried to quiet him, and then again raised her head and called for help. At last she saw Prudence step into the yard and put up an umbrella.

'Come! Oh, come quick! He's dying! Eric's dying!'

Prudence gave one look and then turned back to the house. Sukey bowed herself over Eric's breast and began to cry helplessly. Now he struggled no longer. She was sure he was dead and she meant to die with him. Ages passed. When she heard footsteps approaching she thought confusedly that the grave-diggers were come. She raised her head ; she would tell them that they could bury her too.

There was Prudence, and there were the Nomans.

'Get up,' said Prudence, taking her by the shoulder. 'What a way to behave, crying and carrying on over an idiot in a fit ! '

Part ii

SUKEY's bedroom was an attic. The walls were cut short by the slope of the roof, and in order to look out of the window it was necessary to crouch on the floor. When Prudence had thrust her in and turned the key on her, Sukey had settled down by the window to keep watch. Everything that had befallen now seemed immeasurably far off, and she saw the events of the morning like something happening on a distant hillside to people she had never seen before, like something dwelling in the small round world of a telescope, distinct, soundless, and minute.

Mr Noman had signed to Jem, and together they had carried Eric into the house. She had struggled to follow them; she had caught hold of Eric's hand, which was trailing in the mud. Mr. Noman looked over his shoulder. 'Keep her back,' he said. 'We don't want her bothering round.' Then she had cried out wildly that she loved him, that he was hers to tend and no one else's, that it was cruel, cruel to keep her from her love. And then, suddenly becoming aware that they had gone indoors, and that there was only Prudence left to hear her entreaties, she had locked up her lips and given her whole attention to trying to twist out of Prudence's grasp. Prudence gripped her shoulder with her right hand, with her left she tried to hold up the umbrella. At first she laughed and taunted Sukey, then she lost her temper and thrust the umbrella down over her, bowing her head with it, enclosing her beneath the roof of a black trap. But a gust of wind caught it, twitched it sideways, and blew it inside out. 'Damn you!' Prudence said, and stamped on Sukey's foot. The ground was muddy; for a moment she staggered, and in that moment Sukey wrenched herself free and ran towards the house, towards Eric. In the back-kitchen doorway she collided with Mr Noman.

'Now, Sukey, what's all this?'

His voice was stern, but it was not unkind, he was not going to mock her as Prudence had done; and this unnerved her, so that she could find no words, she could only hold up her hands to him.

'Take care she doesn't scratch your eyes out,' came Prudence's voice behind her. 'Such a young wild-cat I never did see. And would you believe it, she's chopped that bird for all I told her to stick it. Defied me flat, she did. Any one would think the girl was gone out of her senses.'

Mr Noman paid no attention to Prudence. He looked searchingly at Sukey and repeated his question. She struggled for speech, but she could only find one word :

' Eric ! '

' If you mean young Mr Seaborn, you know already what has happened to him. He has had a fit. And as far as I can understand, it is your doing.'

' Yes, I 'll be bound it is,' Prudence broke in. ' For the artful little piece has been tagging round after him I don't know how long. I got it out of her only this morning that yesterday she and him was out on the marsh together, and not for the first time neither, I 'll be bound. Pretty London ways, to go sneaking out after dark with an idiot.'

She had turned on Prudence.

' If you say that again, I 'll kill you.'

' Now, Sukey, none of that. What Prudence says is true. Young Mr Seaborn is not in his right mind, never has been, never will be. He 's harmless, and that 's all you can say for him. Mrs Seaborn keeps him here because when he 's in the rectory he pines. And what she 'll say when she hears of this morning's work I don't know.'

The walls were going round her. The passage was full of smoke. In another moment the wind would lift up the whole house and carry it away and she would be left standing alone on the marsh. She straightened herself and said in a dead, desperate voice :

' I don't care if he is an idiot.   I love him.'

Mr Noman said to Prudence :

' Take her up to her room and see that she stays there.'

Now she crouched on the floor, keeping watch. Her window looked out over the front porch.   It commanded both the path up from the creek and the track which led away to Dannie ; no one could come to New Easter or leave it without her knowledge.

She had not watched for long before something happened.   Reuben, wearing an oilskin coat and a sou'wester, had come from the stable, leading the white horse, had mounted and ridden down to the landing-place.   She saw him guide it, splashing and slipping, through the channel, she saw him urge it up the steep bank of the sea-wall.   That meant that he was riding to South-end by the short way, that he was riding in haste for a doctor.

She watched and waited.   The noise of the wind and rain prevented her from hearing any-thing that was going on in the house, and the only other sound that came to her ears was the tick of the alarm-clock which she had fetched

from the chest of drawers and set down beside
her for company. The dark day began to darken
further into evening. While she had been looking out of the window the remaining leaves on
the currant-bushes at the bottom of the garden
had all been plucked away, and the puddles on
the front path had spread and mingled into a
pond. It was nearly five o'clock, and the
cockerel had been put into the oven—for her
sense of smell, sharpened by hunger, had caught
the odour of baking meat—when she saw something approaching along the track from Dannie.
As it came nearer she saw that it was a closed
carriage, a brougham, very spick and span, drawn
by a high-stepping bay horse and driven by a
coachman with a cockade in his hat. The coachman touched the horse with his whip. It began
to trot faster, and the brougham undulated over
the uneven ground while the water splashed up
from the horse's hoofs and the merry wheels.
It turned in at the gate and drew up just under
her window. She saw the coachman jump down
from the box and open the brougham door. A
lady stepped out, wearing a fur-trimmed mantle
and carrying a muff. The light from the parlour
window shone full upon her, upon Mrs Seaborn,
beautiful as only beauty can be when one sees it
again and salutes a perfection transcending the

scope of memory. And in an instant she had passed in under the porch and was gone.

The coachman threw a cloth over the horse's loins, then he struck a match and lit the carriage-lamps. The two rays of light strengthened and streamed out, mistily enlarging, through the dusk that they confirmed as darkness. A myriad splinters of rain seemed to be suspended in their beam, the grass they illumined showed its every blade, and among the shadowy bulks of the rick-yard hovered two ghostly moons. The horse twitched its ears, shivered and fidgeted. The coachman climbed on to the box again and sat there impassive, like an idol. Jem came out and looked at the horse, then he walked slowly round to the back of the brougham and stared at it with interest. The coachman did not even glance at him.

All along the marsh the wind was rumbling and booming, a hollow noise like thunder's ghost. But it was defeated now, it was dying down, the pressure of the thick night was flattening its wings, bearing down on it, compelling it to crawl along the earth like a maimed dragon. Every now and then it gave another flap with its giant wings and the farmhouse shivered at the blow, but on the sides of the rain-sodden ricks where the two moons hovered, livid, putrescent, coloured like the corruption of light, scarcely a straw moved. Everything was heavy and resigned with rain.

Tired of being an onlooker, Jem had gone in again. The horse shook its head impatiently, mouthed the bit and struck the ground with its fore-hoof. In a sudden flash of recollection Sukey remembered the afternoon in late July when she had sat on her tin box in the rectory stable-yard, waiting for Mr Noman to take her to New Easter. How hot it had been, and yet she had felt rather cold and unreal, chilled with hunger, with the fatigue of anxiety, and with emotion. The tarnished lime-blossoms had breathed their death-sweet into the air, the doves had flown from bough to dovecot, from dovecot to bough with a soft, abrupt clatter of wings, and she had sat, motionless, inattentive, while there welled up in her, pure and sad, passionate love for Mrs Seaborn, passionate trust, passionate compliance and meekness, the adoration, pure and sad, of mortal clay for a creature of light. Ah, no wonder she had so worshipped her, the beautiful mother of her love! Crouched on the floor in cold and darkness, Sukey rocked herself softly to and fro, whimpering like a child that is comforted and taken back again into kindness. Her body ached no longer, the blood began to flow evenly through her cramped limbs, her parched throat and hot eyes forgot their pain, the cold, stifling grip upon her heart slid away and released her. The thought of Mrs Seaborn covered her with the warmth of wings. Mrs Seaborn, so beautiful, so harmonious, so full of gentle deeds and lady graces, was the mother of her love. She would understand, she would be gracious, she would succour them together, Eric and Sukey, pitying their childishness which had strayed into the grown-up severity of love. She would not mind about the baby. She would know what love is.

I don't look to be made a lady of, thought Sukey, for that I could never be. I am Sukey Bond, and must stay what I am. Even if I had been to church and come out Sukey Seaborn, that wouldn't alter me, it would only be a new name in the register. But Eric is not quite a gentleman, he would never do to lead a gentleman's life. Mr Noman said that Mrs Seaborn sent him here because he pined in the rectory. Perhaps it is even as well that I am not a lady. For since my poor dear is an idiot, he might not find a lady to marry him, and even if he did, she might scorn him, like Michal scorning David in her heart when she looked out of the window and saw him dancing. If I saw Eric dancing, I would dance with him. No, Mrs Seaborn won't expect us to live in Southend, where there would be no cattle for Eric to look after, and no lambs for him to laugh at, but strangers to make him feel shy and gentry ways to bind him, and where he would have to wear a tall hat. She will understand that, she will let us live in the marsh. A little cottage, with pointed windows and a bright red chimney-pot. . . . We would keep a cow, two cows, a little dairy. And then I would make the rectory butter, I would make it fresh every day. And we would keep white Leghorn fowls—their slim, pointed eggs are the sweetest of all—and a gentle dog that need never be chained up.

' Oh, I *would* make him happy,' she said aloud.

The coachman turned his head, so that for a moment she thought that he must have heard her. But it was other voices he heard; she heard them too, and pressed herself against the pane. There was Mr Noman, putting up an umbrella, and Prudence spreading a strip of carpet over the puddled path. Now came Jem carrying a port-manteau, which he put into the brougham. They were taking him away; Mrs Seaborn was taking him back to Southend. How was he? Was he still as she had seen him when he was carried into the house, his hand trailing to the ground, his lips discoloured and slack ?　But when he appeared, Eric was walking, and though his mother led him by the hand, he seemed well able to walk alone, for his gait was just as it ever was, light and free.　His face was hidden from her by the canopy of the umbrella.　But she was to see him clear for a moment, for while Mrs Seaborn was getting into the brougham he turned a little back, and stood motionless, looking up at the house as though he were at a loss. Mrs Seaborn's hand beckoned from the darkness of the brougham.　Mr Noman touched him on the shoulder.　Docile and smiling, he came back to life and jumped in after her.　Mr Noman tucked in the rugs and closed the brougham door. The coachman gathered up the reins.　They were off.

A thought flashed up in Sukey's mind.　When Eric turned back and looked up at the house, was he looking for her ?

She struck her hand through the pane.

' Good-bye, my darling, good-bye !　I will soon come after you.'

But it was too late.　The horse, glad to be moving, was going at a trot, and the brougham was now but a black box, sealed up, lurching onward into the darkness with a rather jaunty motion, while its two beams of lamplight wavered before it like antennae. He could not have heard her.

The moist air rushed in at the broken window. It struck upon her face with an extraordinary reality, arousing her, intoxicating her with a violent consciousness of her own existence. The noise of the broken glass tinkling on the flag-stones below still rang in her ears like a chime; she half thought that it was falling still, and that the house was falling with it, the walls sinking from around her, slowly sinking into the earth, while she was floating upwards, gathering buoy-ancy with each mouthful of fresh air she drew. In this moment everything became perfectly clear, perfectly easy. She knew what she wanted, and that in order to get it she must act. All her life long, up till now, the future had been to her an uncertain dream, an uncharted region of cloud, to whose joys she had no claim, over whose terrors she had no control, a state of life to which it might please God to call her. Now she saw it as a road along which she must walk at her own will. What difficulties she might meet and how she should overcome them she did not know, but she would meet them as difficulties, going towards them with an intent; she would not await them as one awaits dreams, submitting oneself to sleep, borne passively towards them;

and thus met, they could be overcome. The small act of breaking a window-pane had taught her all this. A year ago, a month ago, even a day ago, she could no more have struck her hand through a pane of somebody else's glass than she could have flown. It would have been there with an eternal and separate being, a thing set, like the bounds of the sea, a transparent wall between her and her desire ; and now she had put out her hand and brushed through it, and the melodious noise of its falling still chimed in her ears, and the moist air flowed in at the breach, and circled round her, congratulating her, fawning upon her because she was so strong.

What had the Nomans thought ? For they must have heard it fall, must have seen her hand signalling through, while they watched the brougham drive away. They were not so likely to fawn. She laughed. Poor Mr Noman would never take another orphan into his service ; she must have shaken his faith in orphans. Her thoughts played upon him with tenderness, poor Mr Noman !—for he was the first difficulty to be overcome, the first step on her road to Eric, and for that she needs must love him. When would it begin, this overcoming ? How much longer was she to be locked up in the attic, like a naughty child that can be put out of the way until it has ceased to be a nuisance? She jumped up and began to walk up and down the room to warm herself, taking pains that each step, proud and pouncing, should abet her sense of powerful impatience, admiring herself for walking so like a wild-cat. Even though she should break more glass, she could not jump out of the window. It was too small.

She was still enjoying her walk when the staircase creaked under footsteps, and the light of a candle shone through the chinks of the door. The lock turned, and Prudence came in, carrying a tray with some food on it.

'You're to eat this,' she said, 'and then you're to come down and speak to Mr Noman.'

Sukey stepped forward into the light of the candle.

'Oh, so you've stopped crying, have you? Perhaps you've come to think that an idiot isn't worth making such a mighty fuss about after all.'

Sukey looked at the food on the tray.

'Why, Prudence, I do think you might have brought me up a bit of that cockerel.'

Prudence turned about with an angry stare, but Mr Noman must have charged her not to speak with the culprit, for, setting down the tray with a flounce, she left the attic in silence.

In the parlour was Mr Noman, sitting alone

and wearing his best suit. His look was cross and careworn, and as Sukey entered the room he was mopping his forehead with his Sunday handkerchief. Seeing her, he thrust the handkerchief into his pocket, straightened himself into a judicial attitude, and said :

' Now then, Sukey, what have you got to say for yourself ? '

' If you please, sir, I wish to give notice.'

' Dang ! ' exclaimed Mr Noman with the utmost spontaneity.

Sukey felt a small close tremor racing over her limbs. She trembled, not at Mr Noman, but at the instant success of her attack. Mr Noman was never heard to use bad language ; he had threatened to turn Jem out of the house for swearing at the cat when it scratched him ; and now she had made him say ' Dang ! ' It was almost embarrassing to have got such a bull's-eye at her first shot. So might David have trembled when Goliath's loud roar told him how the pebble had sped to its mark. But she kept her ground, said nothing, and feigned to have heard nothing.

Mr Noman took out his pipe and began filling it, but his hands twitched and he spilled the tobacco on the tablecloth. His face was suffused with a dull crimson colour and he kept on swallowing. When he had filled his pipe, he lit it and pulled at it once or twice, but his look was uncomforted, and after the third pull he sighed and the large red face puckered.

' Why do you say that ? ' he began in a peevish voice. ' Haven't you been well treated here ? And as for to-day's work, you 've only yourself to blame.'

He paused. She felt herself slipping back into the dominion of the old tender conscience, the old docility, but she held on to her resolution and was silent. Presently he began again, speaking, not like an offended master, but as man complains to woman, always so sympathetic and understanding.

' I don't know when I 've been so put about. It 's enough to disgust a man from trying to do his duty by all. I 've had such remarks passed at me this day as I never thought to hear from any lady, still less the lady of a clergyman. And now you walk in at the end of it all and give notice.'

' If you are so put about, sir, I might stay on till you are suited. At least . . .'

He roared with another burst of temper :

' Go when you please ! '

The broken glass was still lying on the flag-stones when she walked out of New Easter farm

88

about noon of the following day.   Zeph was in
the rickyard, standing on a ladder and fastening
down the tarpaulin that the gale had ripped loose.

' Zeph, will you put me across the creek ? '

He turned slowly and looked down on her.

' It puts me in mind of Sunday.'

' What does ? '

' Seeing you in a bonnet.'

It seemed that this would be Zeph's only comment on her departure, but after he had rowed
her across the creek, he looked at her long and
thoughtfully as she stood on the summit of the
sea-wall, a respectable, small, black-clothed figure
against the grey sky.

' So you 've left the island.'

The sky was covered with small, broken
clouds, like broken curds.   They moved fast
with the wind.   Below her was the brimming
creek.   The tide was turned, the waters, swollen
with inland rain, were jostling out to sea.   The
long winter grasses, the bushes of sea-purslane
growing along the water's edge, bobbing up
and down with the water's passage, now sucked
under, now swimming up again, all leaned stream-
ing the same way, seawards.   The waters hurried
east, the clouds west.   Every now and then a
gust stooped and flawed the creek, brushing up a
fine spray, dragging a rapid look of light across

the water. There was something urgent and secret in the appearance of this landscape, so full of movement, so denuded of colour. Only the farm of New Easter remained motionless, seeming almost unreal because of its solid reality, its water-logged depth of colour, planted there so solidly upon its acres wrested from the sea, stubbornly impassive in a fluid world, intact between the contrary tides of hurrying cloud and hurrying water. No, it did not look real, and when a smell of wood-smoke came across the water, Sukey could scarcely bend her mind to the thought that it came from the kitchen fire which she herself had kindled that very morning.

' Yes, I 'm leaving the island,' she murmured, almost to herself. ' Good-bye, Zeph! Thank you for having been kind to me.'

She turned swiftly, scrambled down the further side of the sea-wall, and set off along the track to Ratten's Wick. When next she glanced back, there was nothing left but the rampart of the wall, and that already seemed a long way behind.

Before leaving the farm, Sukey had written a letter for Mr Noman :

Honoured Sir,

 Seeing as you said yesterday I was to go when I pleased I wish to go now, and hope you will not think it A Liberty. I have given the rooms a good clean-out, and the Dinner is keeping warm in the oven. My clothes are packed in my Box, which is under my bed, and please may I leave them as it is too Heavy to be carried, and when I know more I will let you hear from me. But I would rather go now. Also my money, Which you said you would Keep for me as I had no money Box. And Please will you take out Enough to pay for the window I broke, also what may be due to make up for me leaving like this. Hoping you will not think it a Liberty but I would rather Go Now.

> *Yours Respectably,*
> *Sukey Bond.*

Thus, dressed in her Sunday clothes and carrying two clean pocket-handkerchiefs, a clean pair of stockings, and her church money—two-and-sixpence in threepenny bits—Sukey Bond walked over the marsh towards Southend. Her impulse was to run, but she walked, for having as a woman turned her back upon the place to which she had been brought as a child, it would not be enough to act boldly; she must also be wary and sedate. During the night she had meditated upon this need for wariness, though her meditation had not been long enough to allow her to do much more than to acknowledge the necessity, for she had fallen asleep almost as soon as her head touched the pillow, to dream that she was sailing over the sea, very comfortably seated upon an iceberg, and that Eric came walking upon the waves to meet her, holding in his hand a blue convolvulus. He came close; he gave her the flower silently, and her iceberg sank beneath her with a splintering chime, and she too could walk upon the waves, telling Eric that they must certainly have a kitten. Now she was walking in a quite natural way towards Southend, but for all that it was not very much easier to meditate upon wariness, for her steps patted the thoughts out of her head, and the wind, blowing so fresh and gay after the storm, imposed its wilfulness upon her will to be sober. Already she had reached the real road that had hedges on either side of it, and occasional elm-trees by its farm-gates, and yet she had not settled upon the words which were to make everything plain to Mrs Seaborn. She would be left in the hall. . . . No, she would be shown into the dining-room—that was where ladies interviewed girls who were in service—and presently Mrs Seaborn would come in, wearing a grey dress, perhaps—but how beautiful she would look dressed in a rather dark red, the colour of a dahlia—anyhow, she would come in, and on her tapering white fingers there would be gold rings. One of those rings would be a wedding ring. And under her warm chin, hanging from a fine chain, would be a small gold cross, for Mrs Seaborn was the wife of a clergyman, she was married to the rector of Southend. The rector of Southend was Eric's father. How strange that Eric should have a father!

Sukey stopped dead in the middle of the road. It had never occurred to her that Eric had a father. He didn't seem to need one, to be the son of Mrs Seaborn was enough, nothing more was needed to account for him. Oh, dear! Why had she thought of Mr Seaborn just now? The Reverend Smith Seaborn—that was his name; she remembered reading it in a list of subscribers to Miss Pocock's coffee-service. *The Reverend Smith Seaborn*—10*s*. *Mrs Seaborn*—5*s*. What was he like? Had she ever seen him? Quantities of clergymen had inspected the orphanage, and she was never much good at telling gentlemen apart, their clothes were all so much alike. Perhaps it was he who had said that Milly Fisher must be sent away, poor Milly Fisher, who had so greatly longed to be loved by a young man. If so, what would he say to her? She had been ready overnight to meet difficulties and overcome them. She was ready still; but she had not then foreseen that one of them would be a difficulty in Holy Orders.

Resolutely she set herself to walk on again, though now as her steps rang out on the empty road they sounded different, not so merry and companionable as they had been. The road here, too, ran beside a long brick wall, and there was an echo. Her footsteps clattered behind her, and she listened to them curiously, as though they were the steps of some one she did not know, the steps of a girl who was in trouble, hurrying her on with their greedy ' One, two, one, two,' till at last she and her shame stood still before a clergyman, a clergyman she must make her father-in-law. Clattering on, the steps came after her, and almost caught her up. She was glad when she had walked beyond the wall.

' But I am really walking,' she said to herself, ' to see my dear.'

It was strange ; she had come all this way, nearly two-thirds of her journey, thinking forward to Mrs Seaborn and to Mr Seaborn, but of Eric she had scarcely thought at all. Even now, when she tried to wind her thoughts about him, he was not really in her mind, and the embraces of her spirit were baffled and impotent. This unknown she walked toward disallowed all that she had ever known.

Now she was on the road bordered with those elms which had lowered, dusty and swarthy, when she had driven out from Southend with Mr Noman. It was here that he had pointed with his whip and said : ' There are the marshes.' Her journey was nearly at an end. She turned aside into a field, changed her stockings for the clean pair, and wiped the mud off her boots with a wisp of winter grass. The view which she had seen then lay before her. She looked at it, and looked away. She had seen nothing.

Entering the town, she found herself at a loss which way to turn. As she stood hesitating at the corner of the street a succession of heavy iron strokes swelled overhead. The first quarter, the second quarter, and the third. She glanced through a shop window in search of a clock. It was a quarter to three. While she had been walking the wind had dropped, and the clouds had settled together and covered the sky. The last throb of the chimes ceased on the air, slowly, as though it were being frozen to silence. Where there were chimes, there was a church, and close by the church must be the rectory. She knew now which direction to take, and turned towards the place of the sound. It was colder in the streets than in the open country, and the few people she passed looked nipped and sour, but at the foot of the street leading to the church was some one who looked comfortable, a stout woman wearing a white apron and a bonnet with feathers in it, who had a basket on her arm, covered with a baize.

' Here you are, Miss.   Apple pies, fresh out of the oven, and piping hot.'

Her mouth watered. She had eaten some dinner before she left the farm, but now that seemed a long time ago.   The woman held out a pie. Sukey shook her head and walked on. What would the Reverend Smith Seaborn say if it ever came to his ears that his daughter-in-law-to-be had been seen eating a pie in the street ?   Yet she was hungry ; this strange feeling must be hunger, not fear.   If she were to eat one of those pies she would be able to walk into the rectory as bold as a lion.   It might not be sedate to eat pies in the street, but it would certainly be wary, and wariness was the prime necessity.   She turned back towards the smiling pie-woman, towards that delicious and heartening odour.

' Threepence a-piece, Missie. I thought you 'd change your mind.'

One of the threepenny-bits dropped into the pie-woman's red hand as comfortably as though it were dropping into the red bag, and the people going by never turned their heads. A poor girl, a farm-servant out of a place, eating a pie at the street corner was nothing to them.

' Tasty, isn't they ? '

Sukey nodded, for her mouth was full. When she had finished she stood rubbing her mouth with the back of her hand and shaking her skirts, lest a crumb should lurk about them. It would not do to carry any of that pie into the rectory on the outside of her person.

' Shall I do now ? ' she asked this woman, so kind and understanding that it came naturally to treat her as a kind of momentary mother.

' Your bonnet's a bit on one side,' said a voice surprisingly close behind her.

Sukey switched round. The speaker had gone by ; there was nothing now to be discovered of her but a stout, tightly-laced female form, a swinging gold earring, and a pair of black velvet boots.

' Ah, that took you by surprise, didn't it ? ' observed the pie-woman. ' A soft stepper she is, and I daresay from the look of her she finds it useful. I saw her. She 's been watching you quite a piece, but never you mind. Watching never harmed a girl.'

There was something slightly warlike in the pie-woman's manner that made Sukey hasten to say appeasingly :

' Well, it was very kind of her to mention about my bonnet.'

The pie-woman looked affectionately after Sukey as she went up the street, as though she for her part had found it natural to consider her as a kind of momentary daughter. Then another customer came along, and the black feathers nodded in a new conversation, for she was a profuse and friendly being.

Pushing open the snow-white gate, Sukey set foot in the rectory drive. Perhaps it was that the pie, so cunningly flavoured with cloves and ginger, had made her, as she had promised herself that it should, as bold as a lion, or perhaps the attention of the velvet-booted stranger had given a fillip to her self-esteem ; in any case, she found with delight that now, face to face with the unknown, she felt no manner of fear or apprehension. She was able to look at the house quite coolly, as though she were any ordinary visitor, approaching any ordinary house ; to note the sparrows flying in and out of the close-clipped ivy, and the sweltering summer colours of the flowers looming through the clouded panes of the conservatory. She listened, too, for the doves, but winter had made them silent. Yet this was no ordinary house ; under that roof, behind one of those windows, was Eric. Suppose he were to look out now, from his window, and see her ? But no one looked, and that was

City Campus Library

Leeds Metropolitan University

**Customer name: Abdisalam, Fartun .
(Miss)**
Customer ID: 0333738347

Title: The true heart
ID: 7102002895
Due: 27/11/2012,23:59

Total items: 1
13/11/2012 14:15
Checked out: 1
Overdue: 0
Hold requests: 0
Ready for pickup: 0

Thank you for using the
3M SelfCheck™ System.

as well ; it would be best to finish her errand, to dispatch her victory, before the sight of him came to confound her with the realisation of the vastness of her exploit, the sweetness of her prize, the perilous past hazard of having failed, and lost him.

She pulled the bell, and presently a maid-servant came to the door.

' I have come to see Mrs Seaborn.'

' What name, please ? '

' If you please, will you tell Mrs Seaborn,' said Sukey, glorying in wariness, ' that it is some one from the Warburton Memorial Orphanage.'

The maid went away. When she came back again, she said : ' Step in,' and, telling Sukey that Mrs Seaborn would come presently and that she was to wait there, she left her.

There was a blue and yellow diamond in an inlaid tile floor near an umbrella-stand and a varnished card which gave the distances and the correct hackney-cab fares from no. 17 Norfolk Square, Paddington, to such destinations as the Houses of Parliament, Waterloo Bridge, Shoolbred's, the Smallpox Hospital, the Alhambra, and the Foundling. The Foundling ! Sukey turned away her eyes and looked at the umbrella-stand. There were a great many very heavy walking-sticks in it, walking-sticks that looked as though they could be used to strike thundering blows.

She looked further afield. Hanging on the walls were some pieces of armour, shields and breast-plates. She was considering them with a critical eye, for it always gave her great pleasure to put on a good polish, when a footstep sounded overhead. Sukey felt her blood begin to run smoothly, as though some great danger were past. That step, so light and free, her heart knew it. It was Eric. He was here, he was coming to her! She ran forward. But it was Mrs Seaborn who descended the stairs.

Though her step was light, her beauty seemed somehow lessened, dulled. She stopped on the half-landing, looking down into the rather dark hall.

' Are you from the orphanage ? '

' Ma'am, I am Sukey Bond.'

Now her beauty blazed out like lightning. For a moment she stood motionless ; then, slowly and composedly, she came down the remaining flight, her silk skirts whispering after her. She came across the hall to where Sukey stood. There was no expression on her face, no sign of anger, no sign of pity ; there was only beauty, a fixed lightning. She caught hold of Sukey by the wrist.

' How dare you come here ? ' she said, speaking low and swiftly.

'Ma'am, I have come to tell you . . .'

'To tell me? What have you to tell me that I should listen to? To tell me that you have been behaving like a fool, and worse than a fool? That you have no sense, no modesty, no gratitude, no decency? That you have pestered my son into an illness and disgraced yourself in the eyes of all respectable people? That for all the good training you have had, and all the advantages, you have shown yourself no better than any common creature on the streets? I suppose that is what you have come to tell me, but you needn't have troubled, for I know it already, and I have no wish to be reminded of it. Now go!'

'Ma'am, there is more.'

'I have no wish to hear it.'

'I must speak it.'

She had spoken falteringly, but hearing her words, spoken in this strange, silent house, in this crucial hour, she was surprised how boldly they sounded. Indeed, she had scarcely flinched under Mrs Seaborn's reproaches; she had hardly heeded or understood them, too intently aware of the conflict and what hung upon it to heed how she fared in it. For this was no time for fear, no time for hope; she must speak out what she had come here to say.

She lifted her eyes to Mrs Seaborn's face. In these ruthless looks confronting her she could yet distinguish the countenance in which she had put her trust, Mrs Seaborn, gentle and benign, to think of whom had covered her with the warmth of wings. That was the real Mrs Seaborn, Eric's mother, a being of serener clay, an unvexed fountain of benignity and gracious power, whose white hand could dispense wonders; this other, whose burning fingers pinched her wrist, whose cold tones clattered in the silent hall like a hailstorm, was a mistake, was a distortion foisted upon her by the sleight of some bad dream: to accept her would be an impiety. Sukey bowed her head. She would not allow the credulity of her eyesight to alarm her into treachery; she called in all her senses lest they should bear false witness against the true Mrs Seaborn whom she now implored.

'O ma'am, you must please forgive my boldness in coming here. I had to come, for there is no one but you that can help me, there is no one would understand about love so well as you. It is quite true that I love your son. But I am not so bad as you might think me. I never set out to entrap him, there has been no presumption in my love. Indeed, to begin with I had no notion what it was, what was happening. I fell in love as though I were falling asleep. And now——O ma'am, I do love him so very dearly.'

She paused, she waited, she dared not raise her eyes ; that other, that cheat put upon her by the bad dream, might still be there. There was a long silence ; at last Mrs Seaborn said very smoothly :

' Fool ! '

' If that were all, ma'am, if my own love were all, I would not have come here. I know my place, I know that I am only a servant-girl, and that your son is a gentleman. I would have said nothing about it, I would have gone on alone. But it isn't only *my* love : Eric loves *me*. So I had to come here after him. I couldn't fail *that*! '

This time, though she waited even longer for a word, Mrs Seaborn said nothing. Sukey found that she was looking at the hem of Mrs Seaborn's dress ; it lay unstirring on the stone floor, like the drapery of a waxwork.

' When they told me yesterday that he——that he was not quite like other people, it cut me to the heart. I thought——for a minute or two I thought : Let me die, the sooner the better. But then I thought of him, the poor dear, and how in spite of his misfortune he had loved me. How could I die, how could I be so heartless as to fail him——him who, being as he is, has a hundred times more need of loving than some ordinary person in his right mind ? It would be like failing a child or some poor dumb creature. O ma'am, you, being his mother, must feel this. You must know that, being as he is, through no fault of his own, it ought to be made up to him with more love, you cannot be offended because I love him too. Let me do what I can for him, let me try to make him happy. I would work myself to the bone for him, there is nothing that I would not do for his sake. The day before yesterday he asked me to marry him. He thought we could climb into Dannie church by the window and be married out of hand. I know he wants me, I know I could make him happy. I believe there is nobody in this world who could love him quite as I do. They might be as sorry for him, perhaps ; but I would be proud.'

During this speech Mrs Seaborn had let go of Sukey's wrist. Now she said :

' I do not understand what you think you are doing here. If you suppose that anything you have said is of the slightest interest to me, you are much mistaken. I have told you already to leave my house. It is a pity that you did not do as you were bid, for badly as I thought of you then, you have contrived to make me think worse of you now.'

She walked over to the front door and opened
it. A cold air streamed in, a bleak daylight shone
full upon her, upon the other Mrs Seaborn, no
bad dream now, but the reality, as real as a stone.
She never looked at Sukey. She turned the fixed
lightning of her beauty upon the garden, where
the sparrows were still flying about, where the
solid masses of evergreens stood like dark tombs.

Cowed by that dignity, Sukey began to move
towards the door, following the direction of that
glance so coldly, inattentively, unswervingly
directed into the garden. She moved slowly,
against her will. She had failed, she knew it, but
the fulness of her misery was perplexed by a
feeling that there was something important which
she had left unsaid, left undone. Whatever it
was, it could not redeem her failure now, yet it
might have helped her, it might have made all
the difference—and she had forgotten it. This
troubled her. It seemed to augment her defeat
that she should go from the house to which she
had come thinking of victory, thus incompletely
defeated.

Yet she continued to move towards the door,
dragged on by that unseen gaze, and presently she
had set foot on the blue and yellow diamond
where she had stood waiting, between the umbrella-stand and the card giving the hackney-cab

fares from 17 Norfolk Square to the Smallpox Hospital, the Alhambra, and the Foundling. She remembered. She stayed herself, standing exactly where she had stood then. Now she could lose all, now her defeat could be consummated. She spoke meekly, as if knowing beforehand that there could be no virtue in her words.

'I am very sorry that there was nothing in what I could say, ma'am, fit for you to take an interest in. But I came here to tell you everything, and there is still one more thing for me to tell. Perhaps it will only be nothing to you. But I think I am with child.'

Mrs Seaborn turned back, shutting the door behind her, shutting out the grim garden, shutting out the daylight, shutting out escape. The sound of her swishing skirts seemed to rise up all round like the hiss of water beleaguering a rock.

'What's that you say?'

Her voice had entirely changed; it had come alive, it glowed with excitement and rapacious joy.

'What's that you say?'

Entangled in sudden fear, Sukey found herself beginning desperately to hope. She heard her voice almost whining in its effort to be ingratiating.

' Yes, ma'am, I am with child. Oh, think ! You will be its grandmother.'

Mrs Seaborn's ringed hand ſtruck her a blow across the mouth. She shrank backwards, collided with something that clattered and bruised, loſt her balance and fell. A mouth of darkness opened to swallow her up. While it was opening and closing around her in rings of darkness and semi-darkness, she heard Mrs Seaborn calling out :

' Grieve ! Grieve ! Rew ! Come here, I want you ! '

Two maid-servants came running. Mrs Seaborn pointed to Sukey and said :

' Take this creature and turn her out at the door—the back door.'

They hauled her up by the shoulders and led her down a ſtone-flagged passage which was cut off from the hall by a green baize door. As this door swung to behind them, Sukey heard one say to the other in a low voice :

' Pretty doings for a reĉtory ! '

The passage was warm and smelt of cooking, and there seemed to be no end to it. A row of bells hung along one wall, all the many bells of this house wherein her loſt love was somewhere concealed. The mouth of darkness began to close upon her again. She ſtumbled, and the younger maid-servant gave her a jerk and said :

' Hold up, you ! '

' Gently now,' remonstrated the other. ' The girl's ready to flop right off, and no wonder. So 'd you be if you was in her place.'

' In her place, indeed ! What do you take me for ? '

' I don't call it human. And I 've a good mind to fetch her into the kitchen and give her a good cup of tea.'

' You 'll catch it if she finds out.'

' Don't care if I do. I 'm not in love with this situation. As for old Smithy, I 'm sick of the sound of his boots. Come on ! Let 's take her in.'

Gradually the remembered kitchen settled into place before Sukey's eyes. There hung the shining instruments, and the row of graduated dish-covers ; there was the cat asleep on the rag rug, and there, ranged along the mantelshelf, were the five copper jelly-moulds like temples. There, too, was the cook—she remembered her now—who presently came over to her with a cup of tea in her hand.

' You drink up this,' she said. ' You 'll feel better then. Why, aren't you the girl that come here to go to Noman's ? '

Sukey nodded.

The cook stared at her for a minute, then she

went back to the kitchen table, where she and the other servant began picking over currants and talking to each other. They were talking about her, she knew, for every now and then they would look at her, curiously, but it was nothing to her what they said. She sipped the hot tea, pressing her bruised lip to the smooth rim of the teacup. The warmth of the room, the repose of sitting in a chair after having been on her feet all day, the occasional subsiding stir of the coals, the murmuring voices of the two servants, and their domestic occupation all soothed her and ministered to her, so that she felt herself sinking into a sort of dismal comfort.

'It must have been in July,' the cook was saying. 'No, August. No, it was in July, because I was making the greengage jam. Or was I salting runner beans? Well, anyway, in she climbed, she and her box, and off they went.'

'Looks almost as though she 'd sent her there on purpose.'

'Well, so it does, in a way. Still, I shouldn't think so. Because if you come to think of it, she must have been pretty thick with those Nomans, keeping him there on the Q.T. like that. How sly she 's been over it! So if there was a place going there, she 'd naturally oblige with one of her orphans. She 's always stowing away those orphans. But if she did send her there on purpose—well, she's got what she wanted.'

'Fancy an idiot getting a girl that way,' remarked the housemaid, filling her mouth with currants. 'I shouldn't have thought it hardly possible.'

'Oh, they're wonderful at it. Like the blacks. If you must wolf all the currants, all I say is, wolf those you 've picked over yourself.'

'Well, I call it disgusting. Do you suppose the child will be wanting too ? '

'Shsh ! She 'll hear you.

'Do you feel better now ? ' she inquired, raising her voice.

'Yes, ma'am. Thank you for that tea. I think I 'd better be getting along.'

'Wait a bit, girl, wait a bit. What are you in such a hurry for ? '

Now she had left her currants and stood in front of Sukey's chair, straddling before it, and looking down at her in a way that made Sukey feel encumbered.

'Look at your lip,' she said. 'Swelled right out. You 'd better let me sop some vinegar on it.'

'No, thank you, it doesn't matter. I mustn't stay.'

'Is that where she hit you ? Well, I must say

you asked for it, calling her a grandmother flat
out.'

'Why, were you listening?' She spoke
hastily, too much upset by this to choose her
words.

'I don't know what you mean by listening, but
a door has two sides to it. There, there, girl!
Don't look so like a cat on hot bricks. Suppose
we did happen to overhear something about your
private affairs, that won't hurt you. Besides,
you can't expect to keep this to yourself much
longer.'

Now the housemaid had risen too and stood
beside the cook. Her face was silly and malici-
ous, and she kept on licking her lips, as though
the currants had stung them. Sukey longed to
be away from the rapt attention of these two
strangers who had overheard her heart. No
doubt their interest was kindly meant, but she
did not like it. It made her feel awkward, and
rather frightened, as though, standing so largely
and closely over her, they might presently begin
to tread her underfoot.

The cook was asking questions again.

'Have you got anywhere to go to, later on?'

Sukey shook her head. She had not remembered till now that she had nowhere to go, and
no money but two-and-threepence. Would two-

and-threepence buy her a night's lodging ? But she was afraid to go to another strange house, she dared face no more unknowns. She thought of the pie-woman who had been so kind. She would feel safe with her. But she would not be there now ; she would have sold all her pies long since and departed. Could she go back to New Easter ? But even if she should find her way there in the dark, even if she could walk so far, for she would need to go round by Dannie because of the creek, perhaps they might not take her in.

'No, I 've nowhere.'

'You can't be long gone, not by the look of you.'

The cook had stared at her so searchingly that Sukey supposed she had noticed a smear of marsh mud on her clothes.

'No,' she replied. 'I only left there about mid-day.'

At this the cook seemed completely taken aback, but the housemaid broke into peals of laughter and nudged her fellow in the ribs.

'You shouldn't speak so coarse, Mrs Rew. She doesn't know your meaning, not if you will speak so coarse and old-fashioned.'

'High time for her she did.'

Mrs Rew spoke angrily, but the housemaid

continued to laugh, and then, turning to Sukey, told her that she was a prize packet and no mistake.

The kitchen was very warm, too warm. Sukey's head began to swim, and to her annoyance she felt herself flushing up to the ears. It was the heat, of course, and the strong tea she had drunk, but her questioners would see it and think she coloured with confusion. It was very ill-mannered of them to laugh like that, and to stand so close to her. She would not look at them. She held her head obstinately bent, and looked out sideways past the cook's skirts at the cat lying on the rag rug, a nice sensible cat who minded its own business, whose blinking glance, though turned upon her, only disclosed two lakes of green light, imperturbable and coldly serene. But though she would not look at the two servants, she could not avoid knowing that they were looking at her, she could not help feeling their eyes crawling over her like bluebottles ; and though she was determined not to speak to them, when they began to question her again she heard her voice replying.

No, after all and in spite of the hot tea, they were not kind, they did not mean well by her. She had better get away as soon as possible—

before the next question, before the cat opened
its eyes again.   But their proximity overbore her
will to rise.   They stood so close to her that
there did not seem to be room for her to get on
to her feet, and their glances weighed her down,
lying heavily on her lap.

A steadfast breathing heat pulsed from the fire.
It was too much even for the cat, who sat up on
its haunches and twitched its ears pettishly.   The
green lakes suddenly contracted and vanished as
the cat yawned.   Staring into that delicate maw,
Sukey found herself possessed by the idea that
she was sitting, not in the kitchen of the rectory
of Southend, but in the mouth of some enormous
and somnolent animal.   In another instant those
jaws would descend upon her, would close her
in.   But what was this other thing descending on
her out of her memory, and confounding her
with some extraordinary resemblance between
the present moment and a moment of ecstasy as
actual as the clogging unpleasantness of this ?   A
green net, a pattern of oval leaves closing softly
round her, as under the pear-tree she drew Eric
to sit beside her and held up her lips to his. . . .
It was Mrs Rew's question that had brought it all
back to her, so that instead of the clashing and
interlocking jaws a sweet net had descended ;
and it was not to those words which she had

heard almost without attention, but to her own anxious heart that she replied, speaking softly and with a smile :

' Yes, it was under the pear-tree in our orchard run wild.'

' Well ? ' said Mrs Rew.

Sukey sprang to her feet. This woman, this wicked old woman with the gloating voice and the greedy, stagnating stare, should question her no more. Crawling under her words, squatting in her silences, was something depraved and abominable, some cold-blooded reptile of the mind. Why had she suffered those questions so long, why had she answered at all ? How could she have allowed herself to comply with this cheapening kindness, designed but to one end— to deflower her sorrow, to paw over in common, turn and turn about, the hapless love which was hers alone. She felt bitterly ashamed now of the weakness which had subjected her, and Eric also, so she told herself, to these prying women, a weakness abetted, not by fear or bodily bewilderment, but by an unworthy yielding of the mind ; for though she had wanted to get away, yet she had stayed to hear more, bird-limed by that murmuring conversation over the currants with its suggestion of some female understanding, some wisdom at once terrible and comfortable, the secret simmering of a cauldron tended and tasted by women alone.

'Well?' said Mrs Rew again. 'Is that all you 've got to tell, dearie?'

'I 'm going,' said Sukey.

Mrs Rew leant over and whispered something in the parlourmaid's ear. The girl gave a start of surprise which was obviously put on. Her mouth opened in a slow grin of delight, and she exclaimed :

'It 's enough to make a cat laugh !'

Then, glancing at each other, the two women began to go off in fit after fit of uncontrollable laughter.

'Let me pass ! How dare you laugh at me like this?'

Mrs Rew waved two limp, expostulatory hands at the furious Sukey. Tears of laughter were running down her cheeks. She shook them off, swaying herself from side to side, and as she swayed her staybones creaked and complained, and her grey hairs escaped from under her cap. The parlour-maid was forcing her laughter into an exaggerated fleering cackle, but Mrs Rew's mirth was so perfectly genuine and whole-hearted that even in her indignation Sukey felt that in a moment she must catch the infection and laugh too. At last, after a desperate struggle for breath, Mrs Rew gasped out in a weak, shrill, squealing voice :

'God bless you, girl, you 're no more with child than I am.'

At that moment a bell in the passage rang violently. Mrs Rew had collapsed on to a chair, and casting her apron over her head she rocked backwards and forwards in a silent agony of mirth. The bell rang again. The parlourmaid in her turn cast herself down on a chair, but sprang up again with a shriek.

'O Providence, I 've sat on the cat !'

Under the apron Mrs Rew reeled and creaked like a ship in a storm ; she flapped her red hands abroad like signals of distress. The parlour-maid was clinging to the dresser and emitting a series of piercing howls. Where Sukey's misadventure had failed, the cat's had succeeded, and her enjoyment was now perfectly unfeigned.

Sukey edged towards the door, but at that moment it opened and Mrs Seaborn stood in the doorway.

'Why are you making this intolerable noise ?'

The parlour-maid turned pale, but Mrs Rew, lost, under her apron, to all save her joke, cried out in a reeling voice, as her mistress spoke :

'A virgin ! She 's nothing but a virgin.'

As Sukey ran from the room, she saw Mrs Seaborn looking at her with a smile.

With nightfall had come snow. It wavered, melting and drizzling down, between her and the lighted shop-windows, seeming, as snow does in darkness, to come, not from the sky, but from a little way overhead, each flake suddenly existing quite close at hand, as though it were snowing in a dream. A sluggish cold wind blew from the north-east, and Sukey heard a woman behind her say : 'Winter's come.' Already some of the shopkeepers were putting up their shutters, although it was not yet closing time, but no more customers would come out on an evening like this ; and they were glad to forestall the ending of such a wretched day and retire to their back-parlours where there would be a well-trimmed lamp burning and perhaps a saucepan of something tasty keeping warm on the hob.

Sukey walked faster and faster, though she had no idea where she was going. She was trembling all over, but she did not know that either. At first she feared that the people in the streets would point at her and jeer as she went by, but no one seemed to notice her in any way. Nor was there anything there for them to notice, for on such a cold evening a girl not too warmly dressed would naturally be hurrying home for shelter, and if she trembled—well, it was for cold.

Soon she was out of the respectable part of the town, and wandering through its outskirts, treading on muddy roads that led past rows of workmen's cottages, standing bleakly against a background of fields and pricking up their chimney-pots like ears. Once a wavering glow of firelight caught her eye, and glancing in through the window she saw a woman taking down a toasting-fork from a nail; but she was scarcely aware of having noticed this until, having found that a tall gasworks blocked the end of the road, she turned back and saw, as she passed the window for the second time, that the blind had been drawn down.

There was a smell of cabbages and of rubbish burning, and somewhere not far off was an engine of some sort that made at regular intervals of time a slow, thudding sound, followed by the noise of a gush of water. A dog, tied in his kennel, rustled the straw as he lay down in a new position, seeking for warmth.

Now that she was away from the lights of the town, she saw that there was still a remnant of daylight in the air, though in the overcast sky itself there seemed to be no difference between east and west. She felt safer, here among the fields, but she still walked as fast as her limbs could carry her until, suddenly, she discovered that she could walk no more, her whole body was trembling so. A few paces further on was a gate standing open where a cart-track turned into a meadow. I will get as far as the gate, she thought, and once I am inside the meadow I can sit down. And somehow she contrived to creep over those last few yards until she was safely inside the shelter of the hedge.

She sat down and began to cry. But it was not, consciously, for her own sorrow that she wept. She had scarcely an idea who she was or what had happened to her, she only knew that as she had come along the road she had said to herself, over and over again : 'Oh cruel, cruel ! ' without really knowing what or whose the cruelty was ; but now she found that she was weeping because of the cruelty shown to wolves. No one ever, ever, she sobbed, showed to them the least spark of human kindness, nor ever would ; no one trusted them, no one pitied them, no one had a good word for them ; the wolves hadn't a chance. And she wept more and more bitterly as she imagined a starving wolf creeping humbly under cover of a snowy twilight such as this to the threshold of a cottage standing alone in the fields. The windows were lit, a pleasant smoke curled from the chimney; the wolf had lain for days in the wood nearby, hearing the woman of the house calling up the dog to come in to be fed, until at last, in desperate suppliant craving, it had come cringing through the dusk to lie down before the door and to howl once, very gently.   But at the sound there was an outcry of fear and hatred; the wolf was driven away—perhaps with stones, perhaps with a shot from a gun —and limping and bleeding it dragged itself back to the wood, to lie down and die—a wolf's death.

Oh cruel, cruel!   Why must people be so unkind to wolves?

In the corner of the field was a pond, a faint mirror of the dusk, and growing beside it a clump of straggling bushes.   Sukey thought that there might be a wolf there, hiding from her in fear because she was a human being.   Presently she began to talk to it, begging it to come out.

'Poor wolf, poor wolf!   I pity you, indeed I do.   I wouldn't drive you away, for I am not afraid of you.   You have more cause to be afraid than I, for not all wolves are bad, but no one has ever been kind to a wolf.   Come, please come! Won't you trust me, you poor wild creature? O wolf, won't you believe that I am sorry for you?   Can't you believe it, poor sad grey wolf, poor wolf in the snow?'

There was a sound behind her, and when she turned and saw something coming darkly towards her through the dusk, she thought that the wolf had heard her and was coming, having taken her at her word. She sat quite still, holding out her hands towards it, her one thought being not to frighten it away nor break her promise by any sign of terror. But it was not a wolf which approached, it was a man, who came close to her side and stood looking down on her.

'What's the matter, my girl?' he said. 'What are you doing here, and what are you crying for?'

If she had not first taken him to be her wolf, Sukey would have feared a strange man; as it was, she felt only a sort of numb surprise at his manliness, and sat holding out her hands as she had held them out to the wolf, but in silence, for to this animal she could have nothing to say.

He put his arm under her shoulders and pulled her to her feet. She reeled, being so cramped and cold, and he steadied her.

'There, there,' he said, patting her back. 'Don't take on so! Why, I don't believe you're nothing but a child.'

She sighed, for she knew too well by her unhappiness that she was a woman. She tried to sit down again, but he prevented her.

'You mustn't stay here,' he said. 'It's settling in for a wet night, no weather to sit on the cold ground.'

Obediently she turned towards the gate, as though to leave the field, but when she saw the road she remembered her plight.

'I've nowhere to go.'

'Nowhere to go? But where did you come from?'

'I came from Derryman's Island.'

'That's a good step. You can't get back there to-night.'

'I can't ever go back there. They would turn me away.'

'Turn you away?'

'Yes, I was servant there, but they won't want me now.'

'Haven't you no friends in these parts?'

'No. I haven't any friends, not anywhere.'

'Nor no money?'

Sukey hesitated. No one was ever kind to wolves, but this was a man; and though he had seemed sorry for her his voice was gruff and from what she could discern of him he looked like a tramp. She compromised with conscience.

'I have a threepenny bit.'

The man was silent. Then he gave himself a shake, like a dog, and said:

'Well, there's a pair of us. I've got no friends either, not in these parts. And as for money—listen!'

Something clinked in his hand.

'Coppers,' he remarked. 'And not too many of them.'

Sukey had left off crying. She leant against the gate, snuffling, and wondering in a bruised way what would happen next. She didn't wish for anything to happen.

'What do you reckon to do?' asked the man.

'I don't know.'

Again he was silent. Sukey watched the ghostly snow falling out of the grey air. Soon it would be too dark to see even the snow. After a few minutes the man seemed to come to a decision. He put Sukey's arm through his and walked her from the field and out on to the road. He turned in the direction of Southend.

'No, no, not that way!' she exclaimed, pulling against his arm.

He bent towards her in the darkness as though he would look at her face. Then he turned and they set off in the opposite direction, the man saying:

'Well, one way's as good as another for such as we. And that's a comfort.'

Sukey walked beside him in a sort of dream.

They fell into step and soon all that was left of her faculties was absorbed in the effort of matching her gait to his. Her hand rested on his coat-sleeve; she fingered it mechanically, sliding her finger up and down the wet ridges of the corduroy. About the man inside the sleeve she thought hardly at all; while he had spoken he was, to her natural docility, somebody to be answered; now that he was silent, he was something to be walked by, a rhythm of footsteps that bore along her acquiescent fatigue, whither, she was too fatigued to notice. There was always the dark hedge keeping up with them and the faint pallor of the wet road going before them, and sometimes there was a tree or a heap of stones by the roadside. Even when she heard music at her side she was some time in connecting it with her companion. He had produced a mouth organ and was gently breathing through it as he moved it slowly to and fro across his lips. The soft rambling sound was not like any music she had ever heard before; it had none of the vigour of a hymn. Continuous and indefinite, it was a noise to hear rather than to listen to. It lulled her, it persuaded her along as though it were gently gathering her up like silk on a reel. She was conscious no longer of the heavy walking rhythm at her side. The man had now become a music.

He put his music aside, unfinished, unapt to any ending, and spoke :

' Look out there.'

She obeyed, looking southward, and uttered a cry of wonder and admiration.

' She 's outward-bound,' said the man.

Seeming in the darkness to float, not upon the surface of any tide, but high in mid-air, the steam-ship, constellated with lamps, glimmering in her own illumination, moved nobly and serenely down the channel, bearing her reflections with her, and seeming to be freighted with light. Sukey received an impression of holiness, as though she had beheld, suddenly made visible in the darkness, the passage of some virtuous soul which, bearing with it the elucidation of all its merits and good deeds, moved unhurryingly into its immortality ; and those words in the Bible came into her mind : *That her warfare is accomplished.*

' She looks like one of those shining ones, doesn't she ? '

' Shining ones ? ' said he. ' Who were they ? But she does shine, true enough.'

They began to walk on once more, and after a few minutes he put the mouth-organ to his lips and was music again.

The road turned inland, and after a while

Sukey noticed that they were approaching something dark and murmuring. It was a group of evergreen trees, and as they passed under their shade, a darkness over darkness, a shade that was partly a low sound of swaying wet boughs, she saw some objects behind their stems, objects erect, faintly glimmering, of the height of a man, and all quite still.

'Look!' she said in a whisper. 'Who are they?'

'It's a churchyard. Those are the tombstones you see. Why, there's something doing inside the church. That's singing, and there's a light in the window.'

'They're practising the carols,' she answered. 'I know that one.' And in a wavering, tear-stained voice, she began to sing:

'While shepherds watched their flocks by night,
  All seated on the ground——'

'Slept rough, they did,' observed the man with a chuckle. 'Though why they should sit on the ground I don't know. Weren't there no lambing huts in those parts?'

'They were the shepherds,' she answered in a rather shocked voice suitable to holy things. 'I've seen a picture of them. They were on the ground in that.'

She raised her face to the drizzling snow. She remembered the picture, the bearded shepherds among their sheep, and overhead a sky full of stars and glittering angels, not like this.

The carol came to an end, and presently the singers struck up another. Sukey knew this one too.

'To Bethlehem straight the enlightened shepherds ran
To see the wonder God had wrought for man,
And found, with Joseph and the blessed Maid,
Her Son, their Saviour, in a manger laid.'

A virgin had borne a child, but not so she, there was no baby for her. And once more the pitifulness of her plight overcame her, and she stood mutely beside the stranger, wringing her hands, while the singers went on with their music, their voices rising and falling in a mournful methodical way.

'We'd best be getting along,' said he, not noticing her distress, for she wept weakly and silently.

So once more they set out along the road, her steps striving to keep up with his, but often stumbling and failing.

'Not much further now,' he said at last. 'There's a shed down this lane with some hay in it. I've slept there before, and now I'll sleep there again. And you can curl up alongside of me. I won't hurt you, never fear.'

She did not fear. Too ignorant to know what there might be to dread, too woebegone to dread it if she had known, she turned at his bidding in at the creaking door and sank down on the hay at the touch of his hands. He massed it up around her until she was almost buried in the sweet tickling warmth, then he sat down beside her with a sigh of content. Presently she heard him fumbling in his pocket, and he put a hunch of bread into her hands.

' Have you got some too ? ' she asked.

' Yes, mate, share and share alike. When you're through with that you'll have a swig out of my bottle. And if you were an old woman you should have a draw at my pipe, but you've not been on the roads long enough to find comfort in tobacco, I should say.'

Thus sunk in her rustling warm nest, Sukey felt a little like a mouse, and sufficiently restored for a small, mouse-like share of amusement at the thought of a Warburton Memorial Female Orphan smoking a pipe. But she drank out of the man's bottle and was the better for it.

She was almost asleep when the scrape of a match aroused her, and she opened her eyes to see a background of hay and wattle, a beam with a hoop of rusty iron hanging from it and, very clearly, the hairy back of the stranger's hand and part of his wrinkled and unshaven face, as he bent forward to kindle his pipe. In a moment the flame was gone; nothing was left but the glow of the burning tobacco brightening and waning with his breath, much, she thought, as his music had done. But the clear view of his red, wet and hairy hand had brought him to life for her, and for the first time that evening she began to feel curious about him.

She was too shy to speak. But presently he began to tell her of himself, saying that he had been in youth a stable-boy to a lord, and then a sailor, and then, not liking the sea, had become a cattleman. But he had lost his place, and all that summer he had been doing odd jobs, hay-making in Oxfordshire, harvesting near Tring. Thence he had walked to London and had taken a turn at Covent Garden, but London did not agree with him, and hearing that there was a carter's job going on an Essex farm, he had come down into these parts. A carter had been en-gaged already, and since then he had migrated from farm to farm, finding little work, for it was a slack time of the year.

He talked and puffed, talked and puffed, and the circle of glowing tobacco brightened and waned. When Sukey fell asleep he was talking about Naples.

When she woke, it was daylight, and through the chinks in the roof she perceived a pale blue sky. Slowly and drowsily she came to herself and remembered where she was and how she had come there. She looked round for the man; there was the hollow where he had lain beside her, but he himself was gone. She discovered that she was clasping something in her hand. It was a little box, about an inch and a half long, and covered with sleek pink enamel, exactly the colour and sleekness of a pink sugar biscuit. On the lid was a picture, drawn in brownish lines, which represented a gentleman leading a lady towards an arbour. The lady carried a parasol, and under this picture was the motto : *Friendship endears*.

In all her life nobody had ever made her a present till now. She could say this without any disloyalty to the apples which Eric had rolled to her feet. Sukey had a sense of proper values ; she knew that apples gathered from the wild, however sweet—though they had been intolerably sharp—however lovingly bestowed and welcomed, could not be described as a present. If she had cared for verbal niceties, she would have called them a gift. She turned the little box one

way and another, watching the light which fell
from the chinks slide over its polished surface ;
she rubbed it against her cheek, she studied every
detail of the picture, every flourish of the letter-
ing ; she opened it, and found that the pink outside was married to a white inside, and that in the
lining of the lid there was a small chip which
disclosed a foundation of copper.

He must have folded her fingers round it while
she was still asleep, round this present which was,
she feared, a parting present. For though she
left the shed and looked for him over the wide
landscape and listened in the winter stillness for
the sound of his music, there was no trace, no
sound. Besides, if he had been coming back,
surely he would have waited to make her his
present then. The manner of its bestowal was a
token of farewell, a handkerchief still fluttering
when the visage of the signaller is already lost to
sight. How very kind of him ! She felt terribly
ashamed now of that christian subterfuge about
her money overnight. She with her nine threepenny-bits must certainly be richer than he ; yet
she had shared his bread, had drunk of his bottle,
had received from him the only present of her
life. She longed to be able to make him some
return, to do something to show her gratitude.
He might have needed darning ; a solitary man

like that would stand in need of darning. She could have bought some wool and a needle and set him to rights. Yet, as she considered him, it struck her that she had never met a man seeming so undarnable, so naturally removed from dependence upon human arts. Perhaps he did it for himself. He had been a sailor, and sailors are always handy men.

I will stay here for the present, she resolved, in case he does come back.

The sun was already high in the rain-washed heavens, and a rich purple colour bloomed the moist hedges. Refreshed by her long sleep, set up by her discovery on waking, Sukey beheld another day with more reasonable eyes. She decided that she must wash and eat. Washing was an easy matter. Beside the shed was an old cattle-trough, half full of rain-water. Eating, unless she were to munch one of the swedes which lay in the neighbouring field, seemed less easy to accomplish, until she remembered the church which they had passed. Where there was a church, there would be a village ; where there was a village, there was commonly a village shop.

All day she waited for the stranger to return, and often among the natural noises of the fields, the lowing of cattle, the bleating of sheep, the cawing of rooks, she thought that she heard his music. But he did not come, and at nightfall she pulled to the shed door after her, snuggled into the hay, and fell asleep. The next day and the next night she spent in the same manner.

No one came near her, and except for the woman at the shop no one spoke to her. Yet she did not feel lonely, nor did she for one moment feel afraid. She so much liked this manner of life that she would willingly have continued in her hermitage. It was healing to be thus alone, and the unlikeness of this existence to anything she had ever known before seemed to set her a little apart from herself, so that she could contemplate her sorrow without revolt or despair, accepting it as if it were part of the winter landscape around her, the meek, sodden fields, the hedgerows of bare stem and thorns. It was agreeable, too, to have nothing to do, and her body's idleness was all the more valuable since she had so much to think of. Now that she might never see Eric again, it was incumbent upon her to make very sure of what had been vouchsafed her, to recall all he had ever said, ever done, to glean over the last four months, to garner every kiss, to store away in her heart's safe keeping every trait, every gesture, every shoot of joy. Even her own illusion must also be tenderly laid away.　She could not cease to love the child which had never lain in her womb.

But she could not continue in this sequestered life.　Already four threepenny-bits were gone from her store, for besides bread and some slices of cold meat she had bought a cake of soap, and in a moment of reckless appetite a bar of chocolate.　She must be prudent and think of the future ; she must obey the law of her kind and seek for work.　It would not do to look for a place in any of the farms around.　The woman in the shop might speak of how she had come there to purchase food, questions as to where she had been during that time would follow, questions which it would be both awkward and painful to answer.　She must go to some place where no one knew her, not a difficult thing to do.　A signpost had taught her the name of Shoeburyness, and by some discreet words in the shop she had learned that it was a sizeable place.　And so, on the third morning, she said good-bye to her hermitage and set out thither.

It was early afternoon when she came to Shoeburyness—a dirty brick town that seemed to be growing dark even sooner than the shortness of a winter's day warranted.　Coming along the road, she had fancied with decision how she would read in a window a card stating that a useful girl was required to apply immediately; or perhaps, even more romantically, assist a comfortable widow to rescue her cat from a terrier, an adventure which would naturally be followed by a conversation in which the widow would explain that the cat had got loose because there was no maid-servant to see that the front door was kept shut properly. What a pleasure it would be to become the keeper of that door, to run along the oilcloth passage, like the damsel called Rhoda, when the bell tinkled, to polish its brass knocker every morning, to whiten the steps, to wash, on Saturdays, the two large, resounding sea-shells which flanked the threshold as ornaments, and also perhaps as tokens that the widow's husband had been a sailor! In that case the cat might well be a monkey. Yes, a monkey would make it all much more probable, for, being of a roving disposition and also sly, it would be more likely than a cat to slip out and hazard itself among terriers.

But Shoeburyness proved barren of monkeys, destitute of comfortable widows (or if there were any, they were all keeping comfortably indoors), and Sukey walked up and down keeping her eyes open in vain. She fell back on her first expedient of placards and handbills. She read how five strong young cart-horses, a quantity of farm machinery, and a bay gelding were to be sold by auction at Little Dennings Hall. If the present farmer was leaving Little Dennings Hall, perhaps the incoming tenants would be wanting a servant ; she might go there and offer herself ; but on looking closer she saw that the auction had taken place over a fortnight ago. There was nothing to be done but to wish that the poor beasts might have found a kind master who would not whip them too much. In other windows she read of things lost : a pair of galoshes, a brown leather purse containing keys, etc., a case of mathematical instruments, a spaniel answering to the name of Shock. And coming to the police-station she read of things found : not Shock, alas !—that would be too much like a story—but an old donkey, a roll of wire-netting, and the body of a middle-aged woman with blue eyes. But nowhere did she come upon a notice inquiring for a willing young girl able to wash, bake, perform all ordinary household duties and help with young children, good references not essential. No, that would have been too much like a story also.

Somewhere in the distance a military band was playing. The music made her feel melancholy. The day was raw, and a dark church with iron railings seemed to frown at her. Yet she had come to Shoeburyness to find work, and find work she must. In her pocket she still had the remaining threepenny-bits; she thought she would spend one of them on a cup of tea, for she was chilled, and loitering about the streets had turned the fatigue in her limbs into aches and pains. Opposite the large church was a small public-house called The Hand and Flowers. The door stood open, and she could see a perambulator in the passage, so there would be a woman there, and perhaps a kind one.

She advanced down the passage towards the sound of voices. A door opened and she saw a room full of tobacco smoke and pimply young soldiers. A very thin woman came through the doorway carrying a trayful of dirty glasses. When she saw Sukey she started and all the glasses jingled.

'And what do you want?'

'Please, ma'am, what is your charge for a cup of tea?'

'Cup of tea, cup of tea!' the thin woman cried out in an exasperated tone. 'As if I wasn't run off my legs as it is, and the kitchen fire dead out, for every piece in the town to walk in here asking for cups of tea. Cup of tea indeed! This is a public, not a cats' home. No, you can't have it. You must go somewhere else.'

At that moment a baby in the upper part of the house began to cry. The woman plumped down the tray across the perambulator and turned to run upstairs. Sukey ran after her and laid hold of her gown.

'Please, ma'am, as you are so busy, may I mind the baby for you for an hour or two?'

Standing on the stairs, the woman of the house looked down on her with a curious expression, awakened and mournful, as though something about Sukey had summoned her from her private discontent to the recognition of an universally extended trammel of misfortune in which they both alike were netted. Then the baby began to squall louder; she twitched her skirts from Sukey's grasp, said angrily: 'No, get out of this!' and ran on.

Sukey still lingered in the entry of The Hand and Flowers. For a moment there had been something in the woman's expression that had kindled her hopes, and she was so tired and so discouraged that she was loth to quench them again. But nothing more happened. Upstairs the baby continued to howl, and voices and gusts of unpleasant laughter came from the tap-room. At last she stole out of the house and went wandering on through the same streets she had wandered through before. If the world was so careworn and so taken up with its own affairs, perhaps she had better not break into the sum which was all that stood between her and the workhouse. Perhaps some one would give her a meal in exchange for the performance of an odd job. Surely somebody in this very dirty town would listen to an offer to clean something. Doorsteps, for instance.

She began remarking the doorsteps as she passed through a notably dingy alley. Yes, there on the opposite side was a house whose doorsteps would be very much the better of a good scrub down. She examined the house, speculating about the people who lived there. The windows were dirty too, but they were muffled with lace curtains, so whoever lived there must be respectable, and fairly well-to-do. She walked up and down the alley, glancing at the house and trying to screw up courage enough to knock at the door with her request. It was hard to decide quite what she should say; she could not bounce out with: 'Please may I clean your dirty doorsteps?' It would be best to lead up to it gradually, yet even so, how was the leading up to be initiated?

While she was pondering this difficulty, one of the lace curtains was drawn aside and a young woman looked out, who presently turned and said something over her shoulder. Soon another young woman joined her. They pointed at Sukey and seemed to be having a good deal of fun at her expense, for she could see them nudging and leaning against each other as though they were overcome with mirth.

She did not like this and was about to walk on when the window was thrown up and the first young woman leant out and beckoned to her to come nearer. Sukey crossed the road.

' Go round to the back and give three knocks,' she said in a hoarse voice. Then she laughed again and slammed down the window.

Nothing venture, nothing have. There was a sloppy cinder path at the side of the house. She followed it and found herself in a yard where some dejected fowls scratched among a quantity of empty bottles. She gave three knocks on the door and waited for the sound of footsteps to come along the passage, but she heard no footsteps, and there was no time for them, for the door opened immediately, almost as though some one had been behind it when she knocked.

Such a large woman stood in the narrow doorway that for a moment she felt almost blinded.

' Step in,' said the large woman in a soft, suety voice, and she shut to the door again with great nimbleness. ' Just in time for a nice cup of tea,' the suety voice continued. ' Come along into my parlour, girl. Dear, dear, what a nasty day, to be sure ! '

This reception, so different from anything she had expected—for to be offered just what she wanted was unexpected indeed—took any words she might have ventured out of her mouth. Propelled along the passage, she found herself shot into a very small and very warm room about which she was too flustered to notice more than two facts : one, that it was more filled with ornaments than any room she had seen before, the other, that by far the most striking of these ornaments was a peacock. Indeed, at the first glance, she took this to be a live bird, perhaps a pet, and involuntarily she started back.

' Lovely bit of stuffing, isn't it ? ' remarked the large woman. 'Lots of my visitors take him for a live one. Now then, sit down there where I can have a good look at you, and don't be frightened of me. You 've come to a kind-hearted one, you have.'

Sukey felt that she had indeed come to a kind-hearted one. She could only account for the cordiality of this reception by supposing that her hostess had mistaken her for some one else. She was much tempted to let the deception run on until she had got that promised cup of tea, but to do this required more courage than she could command, and so, twisting her hands together and blushing, she began :

'I'm sure, ma'am, this is very kind of you. It's very bold of me to trouble you like this, and I would not have ventured so far as to come in only the young lady was so encouraging. But I wondered—I wondered if you could find me some work.'

'Find you some work ? Well, maybe I can and maybe I can't. Times are cruel bad. Still, I'm not one to turn away a likely girl, so sit quiet and drink a cup while I think it over ! '

Sukey did as she was bid very willingly. Meanwhile the large lady—for on a more settled view she was certainly a lady—looked her over with a calculating air as though she were a farmer guessing the weight of a pig in a competition. She stared so steadfastly that Sukey decided that a little counter-staring might be warranted, counter-staring discreetly masked with the teacup and innocent of any suggestions she too might be speculating about avoirdupois. The large lady was dressed in shiny black ; her hair was shiny black also, plastered quite flat on her head and at the back bursting out into an enormous chignon. She wore a gold watch, a gold locket, and two diamond rings which were so tight that the diamonds appeared to be embedded in her flesh. From her ears hung gold earrings of elaborate workmanship, representing caged birds. Her large, smooth bosom was curiously inappropriate to her large, smooth face, which seemed by its expression to belong to a man and not a woman. The expression was deep, bland, and commanding, and Sukey found herself recalling the bishop who had come to confirm the Female Orphans. The bishop had worn one ring only, and that a purple one, and of course he had been differently dressed and without a bosom or earrings, but he too had looked with the same composed and masterful gaze, and had given her a feeling, much as the large lady was now doing, that if it should occur to him to put her through her catechism he would make short (though always majestic) work of her if she offended.

'What is your name?' inquired the large lady, speaking suddenly.

N. or M. as the case may be was the mysterious answer in the prayer-book, but the correct reply she knew and gave:

'Sukey Bond.'

'Who gave you the idea of coming here?'

The first words of this question went very near to unloosing godfathers and godmothers. Penning these back, Sukey said:

'Nobody, ma'am.'

'How old are you?'

'Sixteen and a half.'

'Oh! You're shockingly thin.'

'I'm very strong, ma'am.'

'Parents living?'

Sukey shook her head.

'I'm an orphan, ma'am. I haven't any folk that I know of.'

'How long have you been at it?'

'I was sent out in July, ma'am. But before then I was trained for it at the orphanage where I came from.'

'*What?*'

'The Warburton Memorial Female Orphanage, ma'am.'

Surely something had gone amiss with the catechism; or with the bishop. For a strange look, baffled and discomposed, shadowed the countenance of the large lady who but a moment before had appeared so massively at her ease. Had she already guessed that Sukey had left her first place under a cloud? Had she heard the whole story even? Would this disaster dog her through life? Desperately she tried to commend herself.

'I have had several prizes, ma'am. Laundry-work, fine darning, plain needlework, besides good conduct and knowledge of the Holy Scriptures.'

She waited for these words to sink in. They sank into silence.

' I am an abstainer, ma'am.'

The large lady had looked more and more odd as Sukey went on with her credentials. At this last she said with a snort :

' Well, you 've not come here to be an abstainer, have you ? '

' Oh no, ma'am, not if you don't wish it. But if you could give me some work, ma'am, I promise you you wouldn't regret it. I 'd do anything. Even if you couldn't take me on permanently, perhaps you could find some odd job for me. I 'd clean the windows or scrub down the steps.'

' Windows ! Steps ! ' exclaimed the large lady. ' What next, I should like to know ? '

Sukey also felt that she would like to know what next. She was silent from bewilderment. Her hostess bent upon her a disapproving glance.

' My good girl, don't you know a disorderly house when you see one ? '

As a matter of fact, it was exactly because she knew a disorderly house when she saw one that Sukey had hoped to find work here, but she could not tell the large lady flat out that it was the condition of her doorsteps which had given her a motive for coming ; it would not be civil, it would not be politic to do so, even though she seemed herself so very ready to acknowledge her grimy windows and muddy threshold. Besides, was this quite what she did mean ? The catechism had escaped beyond Sukey's competence ; she felt herself at a complete loss, and the best thing to do now seemed to be to remain silent.

But this was not permitted her.

' Speak up.   Do you or don't you ? '

' Oh, ma'am, I wouldn't be so rude as to say that.   I know how soon things get dirtied in this weather, and I 'm sure everything in here is dusted most beautiful.   Why, you couldn't call a room with that bird in it, disorderly.'

She was answered by a sound as though the large lady were going to explode, and then—there was no end to the surprises of this interview—the bishop-like countenance melted in a grin, a grin that slowly and in silence grew wider and wider until, settling herself back in her chair with the utmost caution, as though she were the vehicle of something unspeakably precious that must on no account be spilled, the large lady began to giggle.

Sukey looked on with respectful bewilderment.

'Lord love you!' said the catechist in a weak voice, and went on giggling.

The door opened and a curly-headed girl looked in.

'What's the joke, Mother?'

'Go away, and never you mind,' the lady answered, becoming for the moment a bishop again. But as soon as the door was shut, she began to heave and giggle anew, and to call on the heavens to inquire if they had ever seen anything like it.

'One of my girls,' she said, nodding towards the door. 'Lord, how she'd scream if she knew! But never you fear, dearie. I won't peach on you. Now don't look at me so solemn! You'll set me off again if you do, and my sides ache that cruel. There, let's have some more tea, and let bygones be bygones.'

Sukey might rack her brains; she could not see what she had said or done to be so extremely humorous. However, one thing was clear—that from proving more and more unsatisfactory she had suddenly been snatched up in a fiery chariot of success; so she took heart of grace, smiled, drank her tea and praised it, and then turned to praising the peacock, for there was no doubt but that the bird was of good omen.

'What a beauty!' she said. 'I've never seen

one before, only in a picture. Why, it 's got eyes in its tail, like.'

'Forty-nine tail feathers,' announced the lady proudly, adding in a tone of sorrow : 'Fifty-two, it did have, only one of—one of my gentleman friends pinched three of them to put in his hat. I 'll never let *him* into my parlour again, nasty, low-minded beast, playing such havoc with my beautiful bird.'

'What a shame, ma'am ! '

'Criminal I call it. Sneaked out of the house, he did, without me so much as noticing, and the first I knew of it was in the morning when I come to go over him with a whisk.'

'Do you dust him with a whisk, ma'am ? '

'Every morning regular. And on Sundays I hair-oils him. You needn't be so plentiful with those ma'ams, young woman. Mrs Oxey is my name, and Mrs Oxey is good enough for me.'

Mrs Oxey's teapot was a large one. It went on pouring out cups of blacker and blacker tea, tea that might rightly be described as a rich liquor. There was a glowing fire, a large Coburg loaf, and a quantity of shrimps, and the room which had seemed for a moment so charged with perils and ambiguities was now become cosy as ever. Sukey continued to look grate-fully at the bird, for she was too respectful to look at Mrs Oxey, and anyhow she had seen several married ladies before, and one bishop, but a peacock was a complete novelty. His glass eyes steadfastly repeated the lamplight, the proud curve of his breast glowed immovable, but his tail-feathers kept up a continual slight quivering in the hot air, and it seemed to Sukey that those eyes were living and watched her. Her good meal and the enclosed warmth and comfort of the parlour were making her feel drowsy; several times she found herself dropping off to sleep and waking up again with a start to find the peacock still flickeringly attentive to her, and Mrs Oxey still talking. Mrs Oxey talked about the ornaments with which the room was so crowded; she appeared to know them as intimately as a shepherd knows the sheep of his flock. Every now and then the door opened and one of Mrs Oxey's daughters looked in. Mrs Oxey seemed to have several daughters; perhaps that was why she treated them so cavalierly, for of course a large family has to be kept in order, and ornaments have to be dusted, and flocks of shrimps— no, sheep—have to be numbered, and peacocks . . . and peacocks. . . . She sat up with a jump: some one knocking and Mrs Oxey rising to her feet.

'You went right off that time,' she observed.

'Now wake up and listen to me. I can't give you work, I 've nothing suitable for you. But this I will do. I 'll let you spend the night here. It 's making a great exception, but do it I will, for you 've given me the best laugh I 've had for months, and one good turn deserves another. Besides, you can't spend the night in the streets. You 'd be sure to get into some mischief or other.'

'Thank you very much, Mrs Oxey. I never expected to be treated so kindly.'

'Well, I can tell you, it 's a bit of a surprise to me too, but I don't see what else I am to do. Now you shall sleep on that sofa—I 'll bring you an armful of blankets—and all I ask is that you don't go fingering my bird——'

'Oh no, indeed ! I 'd never do such a thing.'

'And that you stay quiet here and don't go answering back if any one says anything outside. You 're that sleepy, you may as well curl up at once. I 'll lock you in, no one won't get at you. And you can go off as happy and comfortable as if you were in that Female Memorial you talk about.'

Sukey had never slept so warm at the orphanage, nor so late. When she woke the light was in the room, but she remembered her orders and lay still, looking at the pattern on the flowered blind. She had a confused recollection of waking once or twice during the night. Mrs Oxey seemed to have sons as well as daughters; she had heard boots on the stairs, and once the noise of some one singing to a concertina, and sounds of larking. A merry family!

At length her hostess came in, yawning and complaining of the cold. She brought breakfast on a tray, and while Sukey was eating she inquired about her plans.

'I shouldn't waste any time in Shoeburyness,' she remarked. 'You aren't the sort of girl for a town life. No. My advice to you is, go back to the country. There's plenty of farmers' wives wanting such as you.'

Sukey thanked her for all her kindness and promised to follow her advice.

Mrs Oxey had a leather purse in her hand, which she kept on looking into, as if for counsel.

'Here's five shillings,' she said abruptly, and held out the coins to Sukey.

Sukey hesitated.

'Wait a minute!' Mrs Oxey exclaimed. 'I've changed my mind. Clothes would be better. Now how would you like a hat?'

Sukey knew that she would rather have the five shillings, but she did not say so. Mrs Oxey thrust the purse into a pocket and hurried from the room. Presently she returned with an armful of clothes which she spread out over the furniture.

'Here's a nice little hat,' she said. 'Fashionable, too. Dolly Varden hats, they call them. Got a feather and all. What? Too big in the head? Well, what about these striped stockings? French they are, and stylish if you like. I do like these Paris fashions, I must say. Not want them, not even if I throw in the garters? Here's a pink Garibaldi. Or a pair of kid gloves. Jewellery? Well, perhaps not jewellery. 'Twouldn't be suitable, not unless it was this locket with Mizpah on it. No one couldn't object to Mizpah. Bible word, meaning May the Lord Do More unto Me and Likewise if I Don't Something or Other. Seems a lot for one word, don't it? At that rate Dan and Beersheba would mean a whole Act of Parliament. Come now, take your choice. You shan't go off without something to help you on your way.'

In the end Sukey chose a blue silk petticoat. It was a great deal too large for her, but that, as Mrs Oxey said, was all to the good, and having rolled it into a parcel, together with a lace-edged handkerchief that Mrs Oxey insisted on throwing in at the last moment, she thanked her hostess once more, promised never to forget her, and said good-bye.

' Your stocking wants hauling up,' remarked a voice behind her.

Sukey started, hearing a familiar cadence. The velvet-booted lady. . . . Had that swinging gold earring been a caged bird? Had that trim female form been Mrs Oxey's, compassed more tightly for walking abroad. She turned impulsively, but the door was shut, there was no sign of life behind the lace curtains.

All the church bells were ringing as Sukey stepped from Mrs Oxey's door. It was Sunday. She thought she would like to attend morning service, and passing the church that had frowned at her overnight, but which this morning wore no such ogre's looks, she slipped in and sat down in the free seats just before the service began.

In the flurry of departure she had omitted to pay her farewell compliment to the peacock, and since she was by some mysterious means or other so much indebted to him, the reproaches of her conscience distracted her from the earlier part of the service, and it was only when the sermon began that she was able to settle her thoughts and attend. The preacher was an angry one, and very personal. He spoke of Shoeburyness as a furnace of iniquity, full of evil-livers and evil-doers, with Satan labouring at the bellows to inflame their damnation. Sukey wished that he knew Mrs Oxey, for then he might change his opinion. His sermon was the more discomforting in that he himself was an extremely burly man with a face so crimson and sweltered that he might have come hot to the pulpit from a personal inspection of the furnace he mentioned. Sukey was glad that she was in the free seats at the west end of the church. She pitied the chief citizens of Shoeburyness, whose front pews exposed them to the full blast of the preacher's vehemence, for even if they themselves were blameless, it must be painful for them to hear their town so rudely spoken of at such close quarters. Even more did she pity the one-eyed clerk who sat under the pulpit, for the preacher did not only voice his disapproval, he also thumped it, banging with his fist upon the pulpit cushions as though they were so many upholstered Satans. At every thump clouds of dust flew out and hung above his head in the sunlight like pale smoke. But for all the preacher's fury, no one seemed much put about. Perhaps, she thought, they were all privately remembering Mrs Oxey. Even the clerk sat under the thumps unmoved, except that every now and then he sneezed, and when the sermon came to its end the congregation broke into the hymn with cheerful despatch, and received the blessing without any visible surprise.

'What did you think of him?' asked a lean woman in the porch.

'Ah, I always enjoy *him*,' replied her friend, breathing affectionately on his hat. 'He gives a good pennyworth, he does.'

'That's what I say,' said the lean woman. 'I like to see a clergyman perspire on one day of the week, at any rate.'

'Perspiration's the word,' agreed the hat.

They blocked the way, and, loitering behind them, Sukey glanced round the porch. Hanging on a red baize notice-board was a sheet of paper with a printed heading :

PREACHERS DURING ADVENT.

The preachers' names were written below in rather faint ink. She was moving nearer to read who it was that had thumped, and, to judge by the conversation she had overheard, thumped so fruitlessly—for she did not think that his intention had been to please—when the couple in front moved on, and she followed them out into the streets of Shoeburyness, where three artillery officers with flowing whiskers and wearing caps like small tambourines were desecrating the Sabbath by throwing a ball for a St Bernard dog who trotted mildly after it.

Meanwhile the preacher for the day was crumpling a large surplice into a small bag, and replying somewhat curtly to the vestry conversation of his clerical brother.

' Perhaps you may be more fortunate at Southend, but I can't say that I find the Advent collections very satisfactory.'

' Turkey,' remarked the visitor, ramming in an Oxford hood on top of the surplice, ' and port wine.'

' Ah, yes. . . . Are you sure you won't stay to luncheon ? '

' Thank you, but I must be getting home.'

' I hope you will both come over one day in the near future.   My wife would be so delighted. How is Mrs Seaborn ?   As radiant as ever, no doubt.'

' Thank you, she is quite well.'

' She has been quite a stranger of late.   Indeed, my wife was growing a little anxious. " What can have happened," she said only yesterday, " to dear Mrs Seaborn ?   I do hope all is well at Southend."   " My dear," I said, " you may depend upon it, all is well.   If it were not, we should certainly have heard of it.   The brightest star in the Essex firmament could not be dimmed without our hearing of it immediately." '

' The mare will catch cold if I keep her waiting any longer. I shall see you on Thursday, I suppose, at the Restoration Committee ? '

' Oh yes, certainly. Yes, indeed. Yes. My wife was thinking of driving over with me. She has some shopping to do, or so she tells me. Shopping, you know. One-and-eleven-three— ha-ha ! Might we encroach on Mrs Seaborn's kindness about tea-time ? '

' I will give her your message. But I am almost positive that she has an engagement on Thursday afternoon. Good-bye ! '

Walking home with his rib, the vicar of Shoe- buryness observed :

' I believe you are right, Lucy. I couldn't get anything out of him. But that in itself is a bad sign.'

' Of course I am right,' replied the rib. ' Why, it 's all over the place. I know for a fact that for the last week they have taken in an extra pint of milk a day. Personally I consider it a matter for the bishop.'

' The young man may be a visitor. Still, I must admit Seaborn was suspiciously glum.'

' Visitor ? Fiddlesticks ! Whenever has Bella Seaborn had a visitor, a young man visitor, and not flaunted him in everybody's face? No, no, don't talk to me of visitors! But this I *do* know, that as long as I am on the Ladies' Committee, when the Princess comes down for the unveiling Bella Seaborn shall take a back seat for once, instead of flourishing about with the bouquet and monopolising all the credit for other people's work. Why, it would be nothing short of an insult to the dear Queen to let such a shameless creature receive the Princess. The dear Queen has always known where to draw the line.'

' If it is true, it is certainly very shocking.'

' True? It is only too true. I can be positive as to every detail. The poor creature was farmed out in Northamptonshire. But he escaped—they are always so cunning—and walked all the way to Southend, eating nothing but turnips. And just outside the rectory he fainted and was picked up by a constable, who immediately recognised him by the resemblance, and so rang the bell. I believe the likeness is something quite extraordinary.'

' Poor Seaborn! I feel for him. An idiot son is a sad cross. My dear, has it ever struck you that there might be something a little odd about Seaborn himself? His delivery is very violent at times.'

The rib bridled modestly.

' I understand that the resemblance is to *Mrs* Seaborn.'

The sun shone, the mare trotted briskly over the frosty road towards her stable, the springs were admirable, the carriage was upholstered in a most spick-and-span manner, and after the service the coachman had refilled the metal foot-warmer ; yet none of these things availed to comfort the flustered spirit of the Reverend Smith Seaborn, returning to Southend for luncheon. In his small privacy of blue cloth and ivory bob-bins he groaned aloud and bit his nails.   He also cursed the vicar of Shoeburyness in good round terms as a damned, adulating, long-nosed, prying puppy with a damned ugly wife.   For a moment he was almost tasting pleasure—the natural manly pleasure of despising another man's bed—but the picture of his own wife rose up before him, and the pleasure shrivelled into insignificance. ' I am irreproachably beautiful,' said those full, scarcely-stirring lips.   ' But is it only my beauty which has kept you awake ? '   He groaned again, and forgot the vicar of Shoeburyness.   It seemed to him now that Bella's beauty had been his undoing.   If she were plain, if she were un-armed and undesirable, if she were that ordinary phenomenon, a wife of many years' wearing, she would have been manageable, and none of this unpleasantness would have occurred, and he would not now be chafing at that fellow's impertinence.

He glanced frowning out of the window. The carriage had reached the outskirts of the town, and a girl stood hesitating at the roadside, looking back towards the houses, for overwhelmed by the preacher's eloquence Sukey had forgotten about the blue silk petticoat and had left it under the pew, and now she could not decide whether to retrieve it or no. She did not really want it, but if the parcel were found and advertised, and if Mrs Oxey should chance to read the advertisement, Mrs Oxey might feel slighted, and that would be terrible. Perhaps it would become church property, and be made over into one of those bags that go round a clergyman's neck. It was a very pretty colour, and really much more suitable for a clergyman than for a girl in her position.

'Better *her*!' exclaimed the rector of South-end, for he could see that the girl was pale and under-developed. 'She, at any rate, isn't likely to make mischief. No! It will puzzle her to lead *her* husband a dance.'

Yet the harm did not lie in marrying a handsome wife. Other men had done so, and yet led easy lives. Puny fellows, too, who could not stand up to a fine woman—not like him. But perhaps that was the exact trouble. Perhaps it was his very strength which betrayed him, enlarging and feeding his desires, so that he had gone on as a lover when lesser men would have chilled into a husband and so by inattention and invulnerability gained a husband's mastery. There was an idea for a sermon : a sermon on the subject of Samson and Delilah, a sermon against the presumptions of wives, a sermon which would be very seasonable and necessary. It had better, perhaps, be a sermon for men only.

Pooh ! How was he to deliver such a sermon, he whose own wife had made him a laughing-stock and a puppet ? For it was useless to shut his eyes to the fact any longer ; that prating dog at Shoeburyness had shown him plainly enough what quarter the wind sat in. The news was all over the place by now, and worse than the news, the scandals that breed from news withheld, the suppositions, the hints, the jests and insinuations. Why had he given in to Bella in the first place, years ago, when she had first grown ashamed of the boy and hit on the scheme of hiding him away ? An idiot son is no credit to a man, God knows, but yet it would be better to do one's duty by the unhappy child, and not shuffle him off like a bastard. But that was not the beginning, after all. The fault went further back, went back to the days when Bella must needs indulge the boy beyond all reason. Proper firmness then, and she would not have had the excuse so pat to her hand when she had changed her fondness for dislike, that the boy was unmanageable, and could not be kept in the house. At that time, how remote, how undiscoverable the Essex marshes had seemed ! But the bishop had spoken of Southend, leaning from his carriage while the chaplain came smoothly over the spring grass carrying the crozier case. ' The number of candidates does you the greatest credit. I should like to see you in a larger sphere where your energies could have more scope.' Those were the very words, and Bella had heard them, and had been wild for a carriage and to be a rector's wife. Even then all might have been well if he had been firm, if he had insisted that Eric should be moved to that place in Shropshire. But now it was too late. Nothing could be done. Every nose in the parish was snuffing round the rectory ; his credit was gone ; his position was untenable ; he would soon have to write a letter of resignation, for at least the resignation should come from him. He would not have any nonsense from the archdeacon ; there should be no damned tact.

He would resign. He would mortify himself with a curacy. And Bella should be mortified too, and richly she deserved it. And Eric should live at home, to be a lesson to her. But would it be a lesson after all? For now, ever since she had brought him back from New Easter, declaring that he was ill, she had treated the boy as though he were the apple of her eye, shutting herself up with him, cherishing him with the fixed and frantic love of a jealous woman. She had never shown such love for *him*. He sighed deeply, admitting the last injury of a husband: his wife had never been jealous.

'I am not much to her,' he said, beginning to pity himself. 'Because the boy has fallen down in a fit and cut the back of his head, she must needs fuss herself into fiddlestrings. Does she think the world is coming to an end? She didn't think so when I had my gout.'

He pounded against the blue cloth wall that faced him. The carriage stopped. Leaning out of the window, he said:

'Drive on to the restorations, Williams. I want to see how they are getting on.'

The carriage turned into a muddy lane, lurching and sidling over the ruts, and Mr Seaborn, bouncing heavily, drew out his watch and studied it with a compression of his lips. Since his wife cared nothing for him, there was no reason why he should be in time for luncheon.

The untended churchyard grass was marked with bleached parallelograms where it had lain under planks and blocks of stone, and a wheelbarrow was up-ended against a tomb. In the poor man's corner was a heap of rubble, and there also, broken in two, lay the old font, waiting to be carted away. The new masonry, white and sprucely rectangular, seemed to be too big for the old fabric. Church and churchyard alike had assumed an air of sullen humility, the wilful decrepitude of old men in the workhouse, feigning at an unwished-for questioning to be deafer than they are. The scheme of restoration included six new gargoyles, whose pallid faces looked down on Mr Seaborn, strolling about the churchyard and getting his boots extremely muddy, with six varieties of Gothic sneer. A wind blew, moist and penetrating, burdened with the salt sadness of the Thames estuary, which was visible through a screen of fir-trees. The sky was covered, the day was turning to rain, for the morning's weather had been too brilliant to last. Mr Seaborn's thought tapped the barometer in his hall and knew the glass to be falling. Yet he continued to tread heavily over the churchyard grass, eyeing the restorations with a blank countenance and a foreboding heart. Only ten days ago he had come here and had chid the masons for making so little progress, speaking with the impatience of a patron.

For the restoration had been his idea. He had set it going, he had opened the subscription list, he had shepherded the committee. But now he was ready to wish that he had never set his hand to the work. The wind from the sea blew a horrid foreboding into his heart : suppose that the unveiling should be made the occasion of a rebuff, some slight to him or to his wife ? With this accursed scandal gathering to a head, with every whisperer and slanderer in the place busy about him, nothing was more likely. Some woman or other—all women hated Bella—would go tattling to the bishop's wife about ' the mysterious affair at the rectory.' And then the bishop's wife, a woman too, at any rate sufficiently partaking of womanhood to hate Bella, would inflict a public snub.

A qualm like sickness passed over him. The wind blew with a whining noise round the church, and listening to it he felt afraid. At this moment, thoroughly disliking his wife and ready to dismiss her to lie in the bed which she had made for herself, he realised how irreparably the state of marriage had confused them into one flesh, so that any affront offered to her must of necessity prick him too. He must attend the unveiling ; his pride demanded that he should. But would it not be possible to keep Bella away ? he would not mind what happened to him, provided it did not happen to him through her. He turned about like a bull and launched his large frame towards the carriage. No ! How could he hope to keep Bella away ? Whatever he wished her to do, she would insist on doing the opposite.

As he climbed into the carriage, he stumbled against the foot-warmer, and so he began to think again of his gout. ' If I were on my deathbed I daresay she would not stir a finger.' He leaned back, closing his eyes and abandoning his body to the jolts of the vehicle. Wearied out with a week of anger and bewildered anxiety, and with the strain of preaching to a congregation like so many hassocks, and with pacing about in the cold on an empty stomach, the Reverend Smith Seaborn suddenly felt laid upon him a weight that he had never noticed before—the weight of years. His face puckered in a childish grimace, and he said in a voice childishly forlorn : ' I shall die soon.'

He spoke truly. About three months later— it was the first afternoon that it had been possible to have tea by daylight—Mr Mullein opened the *Essex Chronicle*, folded it to his liking and read aloud : ' Death of the Rector of Southend.'

Mrs Mullein sighed appreciatively.   She loved a good death, and though the best deaths are those of servant girls in trouble who drown themselves in a pond, or of old men who die calling upon the Lord to put an end to their agonies, still, the death of a clergyman is by no means to be despised.

' How ? ' she said on a long cherishing breath.

' Poisoned,' replied Mr Mullein.   ' No, 'tain't, though.   That 's pigs at Paglesham.   Let me see.   " On Sunday he conducted the services and preached, appearing to be in the enjoyment of his usual vigorous health.   Those present, which were both tasteful and numerous, included a plated toast-rack, Miss Evans, a pair of floral vases, Mr and Mrs Pawsey, a case of ivory-handled——"   No, that ain't it neither, that 's a wedding at Little Baddow.   " Shortly after he lapsed into a state of unconsciousness. . . ."   It were a clot of blood on the brain, Emma.'

' Now I 've heard of folk going off with a clot on the leg.   But on the brain ?   No, I can't say I 've known such.   I wonder if it were painful.   Probably not, not if he lapsed.'

Mrs Mullein lit a candle suitably, and took

another child's garment from the mending-basket. After a few stitches, she turned to Sukey.

' Why, Sukey, I daresay you knew him. You came from those parts.'

Halfacres Farm was near Chelmsford, and sufficiently removed from Southend for Southend to be referred to as ' those parts.' Even to Sukey the phrase seemed a proper one. To those who have travelled but little, each new landscape remodels the mind, and here, among a rumple of small hills and woodland, she was no longer to herself the Sukey of the marshes. Soon after her arrival at Halfacres, a heavy snowfall had come like a ratification of her sense of change. Its emphatic silence and mystery was laid upon the past like a seal. For three days she walked, an unreal being, in an unreal world, as though she had been three days among the dead, feeling, not resignation, for resignation is of the flesh and it was to her as if her flesh no longer existed, but a motionless and colourless repose, flowing into her from every rounded hummock and unsullied slope. Near the farm was a plantation of birch-trees. Their slender branches drooped to the earth, weighed down with pellets of frozen snow. She pulled the branches to free them of their load and heard the winter fruits jangle together like a chime. For some little while she

Stayed among the birch-trees, walking slowly and pausing before each, Studying it attentively. They were young trees. Like sisters in a fairy tale, there was neither eldeSt nor youngeSt among them; she thought they muSt be about her own age. There was no autumn in their winter, for their dead leaves were buried under the snow, and this gave them an appearance of peculiar innocence. They were too young for any birds to have built in them; nothing impeded the pure flowing lines of their branches weighed down with the winter fruits. 'You shall have your leaves again,' she said to them, speaking as though spring were in her gift and she could promise it; but she spoke for their reassurance, not her own, feeling in herself no desire for spring, wishing the snow might Stay for ever. Under that universal seal of whiteness and cold purity her love and her sorrow and her illusions lay buried like the birch leaves, while she Stood there above them, quite Still for ever, meekly bowed under the weight of a lovely and alien tranquillity.

The south wind blew and the snow melted, and once more the waggons rumbled along the London road. They went by after midnight, carrying vegetables to Covent Garden market, and about midday they came back again empty, but then she neither heard nor saw them, for she would be busy with the young Mulleins.

'I can't rightly pay you much wages,' Mrs Mullein had said, 'seeing as you have got no references. But you will get your keep and your pocket-money, and it will be an easy place, only indoor work and the children to look to.'

There were seven young Mulleins, all so much of an age that it might have been said of them too that there was neither eldest nor youngest among them. But in no other respect did they resemble a family in a fairy tale, for they spent their lives in catching each other's colds and mislaying each other's handkerchiefs, varying the process with an occasional scalding, festering and surfeiting. They were not nice children, but they were not nasty ones either ; they did not quarrel or steal, and so far as their adenoids would permit them to understand any orders they did as they were bid. Sukey's chief difficulty with them lay in sorting them out. During her first weeks at Halfacres she was continually washing little Louise twice over, once for Louise and once for Ida, or dosing Arthur with Egbert's mixture, or comforting Alice for Annie's tumbles. A double allowance of washing or of comforting would not, she thought, come amiss, but she hurried trembling to Mrs Mullein to report the mishap of Egbert's mixture. What would happen to poor little Arthur? They were such delicate children, too! Mrs Mullein was large-minded; she dared say it would do Arthur good. There was that embrocation Mullein had had for his leg, quite half a bottle of it left; she often wondered if it couldn't be put to some use.

Halfacres was a much larger farm than New Easter, and had a bull of its own, a melancholy and ageing beast whose bones loomed through his baggy skin, but still a bull. Mrs Mullein said that it suffered from asthma. Most of the cows were rather the worse for wear also, and their heifers were gawky creatures; none of them could have held a candle to Mr Noman's Tansy, that wilful pedigree maiden. At New Easter Sukey had made both butter and curd cheese, but at Halfacres the milk was sent to Chelmsford to go by train to London. The milkers were two middle-aged women with scarred hands, the sisters of one of Mr Mullein's labourers. Morning and afternoon they came over the fields, wearing galoshes and dressed in black, milked the beasts in silence and in silence went home again. On Saturday evenings they waited outside the kitchen door for their money, and on Sundays they sang in the choir. They were very religious, Mrs Mullein said; it was

reported of Lydia, the elder of the two, that she
would sometimes pray all night, that she fasted,
wore nettles inside her stays, and performed
other strange popish feats. Sukey was very
much afraid of them, yet a strong impulse drove
her to haunt the cowshed at milking-time. The
smell of the cows, the sound of the milk rattling
against the pail as it squirted from their udders,
the motionless, bowed bodies of the milkers,
motionless and bowed like the bodies of wor-
shippers, the look of the first light or the last light
suspended, as it were, in the dusky shed, took her
back to milking-time at New Easter and to the
first beginnings of her love. She saw again
Eric's head burrowing against the cow's flanks,
and heard his song, his voice ambling vaguely
from note to note, a sound like the first airy
cries of a kettle coming to the boil.

She had been hired for indoor work only,
there was no call for her to do milking, and
when she asked for permission to join the sisters
at milking-time Mrs Mullein had demurred, saying that she might catch cowpox and give it to
the children. Sukey asked no more. Without
further words, and without a scruple, she dis-
obeyed her mistress. It was easy to slip out for
the morning milking unobserved, and she trusted
to the women's silence not to be betrayed. 'I

have come to help,' she said on the first morning ; and sitting down by a cow she set herself to imitate the motions she had watched so often and so attentively. The cow was a staid animal, and let down her milk easily to the stranger's handling. At the first few attempts Sukey was too anxious not to show herself a novice to have much mind to spare, but soon she was able to disregard her fingers and give rein to her fancy. Now I am like him, she thought. He, too, had known that drowsy stir of the arm muscles plying rhythmically through the subdued body, had leaned his head against that wall of flesh and bone, had handled those hot teats. It comforted her beyond description that she should be doing what he had done ; it seemed to give her a warrant of his existence.

She had need of such. Here, in this new landscape, in this new life, with so much to do and with every one taking her for granted, with every day bearing her further into the spring, with every evening muffling with renewed layers of fatigue her capacity to recall the past, she felt sometimes with absolute terror that she was in a fair way to forget. One day, in the midst of stilling the outcries of little Louise, who had stuffed her nostrils with soap, it flashed upon her with an extraordinary unreality that she had once believed herself to be pregnant. It seemed the delusion of a child. Just so, in the old days at Notting Dale, she had awoken one morning firmly convinced that she could fly, and had launched herself down a flight of stairs, to roll bewildered and howling into a clothes-basket. Perhaps her very love had been a delusion too. It had seemed like love, but so had it seemed to her that she would bear a child. One was untrue, so might the other be. For what did she know about love ? Nothing. A farm-servant, very young, very ignorant, had been kissed by a boy who was not quite in his right mind. Louise yelled louder and louder as the soap came frothing from her nose, but Sukey did not hear the yells ; she heard only the voice of Mrs Seaborn saying the one word : 'Fool !'

At such times as these she would make some pretext and run upstairs to her attic. There she would lift the lid of her tin box and look in.

Upon her arrival at Halfacres she had written a letter to Mr Noman, asking him to deliver over her box, and her money, and Mr Mullein had himself driven into the marsh to fetch them away, remarking that it never did a farmer any harm to see how another man managed his winter feed. 'Why don't you come too ?' he had asked. 'It will be a nice ride for you and you can see your old friends.' But she had refused, for at that moment it seemed to her that she could not endure to see New Easter again. After Mr Mullein had left the house, she began to torment herself, and to wish that she had said nothing about her box and her money. For suppose that Mr Noman and Mr Mullein got into conversation about her, or suppose that Prudence was there and began to tell tales? Then the truth would come out, and the Mulleins would turn her away, and she would be once more an outcast on the roads. She spent the day in an agony, and when she heard the trap turn in at the gate she ran and hid herself in the wash-house, stopping her ears with her hands, striving to delay, if only for another minute or two, the hour when she must be haled forth to hear her accusation and her sentence: We cannot keep you now. In the wash-house it was warm, for she had been ironing all the afternoon. It smelt of hot clean linen, it was full of tidiness and good deeds. She looked at the blackness of the window, and thought how coldly the stars would eye her when she was out on the road. If they would only let her stay, if they would keep her even till the week was up! She was so desperately in need of shelter now; she was so afraid. Though she pressed her hands to her ears, she could hear

Mr Mullein's voice, loud and cheerful. He was calling to his children, bidding them come and see what their daddy had brought back for them. Now he was greeting his wife ; she could hear his kiss. Yes, of course, that was how it would be. He would think of them first, and then of his supper. Her affair would come later.

She crept to the washhouse door and listened. She heard the children sneezing at the breath of outdoor air their father had brought into the house, and the grate of chairs being dragged to the table. How comfortable it all sounded ! She waited in her hiding-place until the striking clock told her it was time to take the children to their beds. There was her box in the corner of the front kitchen, but no word was said, beyond Mrs Mullein's reminder to her to rub Annie's chest. After she had washed the children and seen them fall asleep she stole back and took up some mending. Mr Mullein was telling his wife of a murder he had heard about at the sweetshop.

' They do say that the poor gentleman was bruised as black as a——' His eye roved about the room for a comparison and lighted on Sukey. ' I 've brought your box right enough, young woman, and here 's the money in an envelope. You 'd better count it over, to see if it 's all there.'

As she was turning over the coins and pretending to count them, he continued :

' A fine set-out there was there, to be sure. To-morrow's the wedding day. I saw the bride-to-be—stylish girl she is, too—and she sent you her respects, and hopes you haven't forgotten her and says she is coming over here one fine day to see how you are keeping.

' Yes, bruised all over he was, as black as a blood pudding. And the police have their suspicions, but they are keeping dark about it, so as to trap the fellow.'

' How do they know it wasn't a woman ? ' inquired Mrs Mullein.

Sukey took the box and lugged it up to her attic. While her candle endured, she knelt on the floor beside the open box turning over her possessions as though they were something holy. Holy indeed they were to her, holy and kind ; as she took out the crumpled garments, she shook a hundred recollections from their folds. This pink print, she had worn it soon after her arrival at New Easter, and Eric, who then had scarcely spoken to her, had looked at it and smiled, pleased with the colour. Into this apron he had tossed the third apple. That was the bodice she had put on to go to the Dannie churchyard, a Sunday bodice, suitable for her serious purpose, and here, here were the stockings she had darned as they sat for the first time under the pear-tree in the orchard run wild. She turned them over until she could certainly identify among the many darns the darn of that day. She had watched her hand guiding the needle through the woollen lattice, while he lay beside her, his fingers loosely clasped about a half-eaten pear, the wind ruffling his locks. And then, looking up from her work, she had stared for a long time—at his ear, at the freckles under his eyes, at the reposing curve of the upper lip upon the lower, studying him, learning him by heart, so that when she resumed her darning she still saw him in her mind.

The owls were hunting close round the house. The two children who slept with her stirred in their sleep, and one stretched up an arm, the shadow on the ceiling of a giant's hand. Sukey knelt before her tin box and interrogated each happy garment that she had worn in the presence of her love. One by one they yielded up their secrets, their faithful witness to the past. This fruit-stain told her another tale of the orchard. Her teeth had already sunk into the damson when Eric, turning suddenly, had kissed her, pressing her mouth and the fruit together, so that the damson juice gushed out and ran down on to the bosom of her dress. Here was a darker and a heavier stain. And for a while she was baffled by it, till there flashed back upon her the remembrance of candlelight appearing in a dark room, and of seeing, by that light, blood on her hand—the hand she had struck through the pane with a gesture, not of farewell but of assurance.

'Good-bye, my darling. I will soon come after you.'

She raised her head. For all that had happened, those words yet held good.

What she should do, how she should ever contrive to come at him again, was beyond her guessing. Her resolve was no more than a tiny flame sheltered in the hand, a taper carried into a future all dark and unknown, but somewhere in that future she would find, so she taught herself to believe, the stratagem, the train of circumstances, which her flame would kindle. Then the fire would leap up, wild and clear like an outburst of music ; then she would see once more the true face of her hope.

Time went on. The confidence of the oncoming spring daunted her sometimes, for having learnt love through the ageing of the year this spectacle of the year growing young again seemed a reversal and an unravelling of all she cherished ;

but the tin box did not fail her, and even Bunyan's *Holy War*, secluded at the very bottom of it, had a kindly word for her, for had she not once shown some of the pictures to Eric, and had he not said that he did not like books ? Now it was possible to have tea by daylight, and the Reverend Smith Seaborn was dead.

It would have been better if it had been Mrs Seaborn, perhaps. But beggars cannot be choosers, and Sukey, who had a practical mind, turned immediately to considering if any use could be made of Mr Seaborn. She could not go to the funeral, that was already over ; perhaps she could plant flowers on his grave. That night she lay awake and imagined herself taking a place in Southend. No one would know how it was that Mr Seaborn's grave was always so neatly clipped, so blooming, so piously spruce and button-holed, for she would do her gardening in the very early morning when nobody was about, planting the cold primroses in the dewy ground, trimming the grass by moonlight. Others would see the morning glory and comment and wonder. Mrs Seaborn would see it too, coming back maybe after years of absence. ' Who has been taking such care of my husband's grave ? ' she would ask. The sexton would shake his head. Perhaps he might point out a particularly fine poly-

anthus. ' How can I find out ? ' Mrs Seaborn
would ask herself, trailing home her slow black
skirts to tea. Sukey herself was not quite sure
how the discovery should be made. Possibly by
means of a label, for people often plant labels
beside flowers. Then, bending to learn the
name of a columbine, she would read these
words : *From poor Sukey*. And then surely her
heart would be softened and she would forgive
and grant.

By day Mrs Seaborn's heart looked less tract-
able, and the following night Sukey changed the
ending. It was now Eric who came to the grave,
walking early, looking, poor dear, for cows, and
as the first rays of the sun stole among the graves
they would go away together. By then she would
be able to earn quite enough money to keep them
both. They might start a market-garden.

One imagination followed another, and they
served as a sort of comfort, though none of them
seemed really likely to lead to much. But she
was loth to admit that nothing could be done
with Mr Seaborn ; it seemed wasteful that he
should die and she make nothing of it.

She was still trying her wits on him when a
new problem presented itself. She received a
letter from Prudence, written upon scented paper,
sealed with quantities of pink sealing-wax, and

signed with a flourish—*Prudence Noman*.   The
letter announced that Prudence would be as good
as her threat—that she was coming to Halfacres
to see Sukey.   After the flourish came two rows
of crosses, representing kisses.   Sukey wondered why they were there.

She had no wish to meet Prudence again, and
in the bottom of her heart she dreaded the meeting, but the surface of her thought was entirely
taken up with one intention : to wipe, if possible,
Prudence's eye with the superior glories of
Halfacres.   She began to reckon up her forces,
and to plan the order in which they should be
brought to bear upon the visitor.   There was no
doubt that Consort must be kept for the last.
She had a vision of herself leading Prudence
across the barton, saying grandly : ' Perhaps you
would be interested in the bull.'   Consort was
growing old, but he was a fine sight yet, lolling
over the half-door, staring blearily at the sunset,
balancing his head under the weighty horns.   If
only he could be induced to bellow !   As for
the rest of the stock, she had a shrewd idea that
the less Prudence saw of them, the better, unless,
maybe, something could be made of the hens,
which were Blue Andalusians.

Within doors matters were more propitious,
thanks to Godmother.   Sukey had brought with

her from the orphanage a great respect for anything that would take a good polish. She had
been advanced to the privilege of dusting Miss
Pocock's own parlour, and not even the glamour
of the peacock and the battalions of ornaments
had stayed her from comparing Mrs Oxey's
parlour with Miss Pocock's to the disadvantage of
the former. The things in Miss Pocock's parlour were Good : Miss Pocock said so, and
Sukey, who had tended them, knew that Miss
Pocock spoke with justification. At Halfacres
a considerable quantity of the household gear
was also Good : the best brass bedstead, the
linen-cupboard, the centre table and the six
chairs with patchwork seats, the copper kettle,
the cut-glass cream-jug and sugar-basin, the tea-
caddy, and the two engravings which hung on
either side of the mantelpiece. These last represented a style of behaviour and of drapery which
Sukey could not feel wholly comfortable about,
but which she knew, on a general conviction, to
be heathen and to be made allowances for. The
easy airs of the gentlemen in helmets and the
healthy curves of their ladies were the more
markedly heathen by their proximity to the
numerous enlarged photographs of the young
Mulleins in various stages of catarrh and collars
too large for them. Some of these photographs

were not only enlarged, they were also tinted, which is a more expensive state yet; but their plush frames were coming unglued at the corners, and they were glazed with glass that had small bubbles in it, like tears shed by the imprisoned likenesses, whereas the heathen, whatever their own morals, were framed and glazed in undeniable Goodness. There was a third engraving, midway in Sukey's esteem between the heathen and the Mulleins, first in her affections. It had a story which she could understand, and a title which she could read—the titles of the heathen were in some foreign tongue and further obscured by elaborate copper-plate scrollings. The title was: *The True Secret of England's Greatness.* The story was simple, but at the same time magnificent. Queen Victoria stood on the steps of her throne, as upright as a pillar-box. Round her, at a lower level and in a suitable shading of perspective, were grouped statesmen, courtiers, field-marshals, bishops, pages, and ladies-in-waiting. At the foot of the throne knelt a negro, a heathen obviously, but how different from those other heathen, for with her gloved hand she was extending to him the gift of a Bible. Sukey would stand in front of this picture and sigh. She wanted to marry Eric beyond all things, but she had also a natural wish to go to court.

The brass bedstead, the linen-cupboard, The True Secret of England's Greatness, etc., had not been all at once revealed to Sukey for the meritorious works they were. Their goodness had been revealed to her gradually—revealed by cleaning. Mrs Mullein was too maternal to be house-proud. When Sukey had observed, regretfully, upon the dints in the legs of the six patchwork-seated chairs, Mrs Mullein replied : ' There 's one thing I do thank Providence for, and that is that all my children are hearty kickers.' Launched upon this grateful theme, she proceeded to some motherly relations as to the date at which this family talent had first been manifested. Sukey went on polishing.

' Lor', girl, any one would think those legs were flesh and blood, the way you fondle them.'

' Such handsome chairs, ma'am. It 's a pleasure to give them a good rub-up.'

' Handsome would you call them ? Bit old-fashioned for my taste. Godmother give 'em me five years ago come Whitsun, just when I was getting about again after Annie. And no sooner did they come into the house when Egbert started to point at their backs and say : " Corn ! Corn ! " He always was a wonderful child to take notice.'

Further admirations produced the same an-

swer : Godmother. Sukey was impressed, and
began to build up in her mind a picture of what
this splendid godmother must be like. She
studied the patchwork seats, wondering if they
had been put together from the remnants of
Godmother's dresses. There was a great quantity of patterned stuffs among them, chintzes and
figured calicoes. Godmother must have a liking
for growing things ; there were so many patterns
of leaves or flowers or berries. The joins were
all worked over with green feather-stitching, and
one afternoon when Ida had been dosed with
salts and was fretful, Sukey had amused the child
with a pretence in which all the green feather-
stitchings were green hedges, each patch a field :
here a crop of yellow barley, here a field of
clover, here an apple-orchard. Ida was a practical child. She pointed out that barley and apple-
blossom would not come at the same time of
year.

During the week before Prudence's advent
there was no time for fancying over patchwork.
She scrubbed and brushed and polished, and got
up the best tablecloth three times before she
could be satisfied with its gloss and crispness.

'Why, you aren't spring-cleaning yet, surely?'
Mr Mullein inquired, finding her busy in tacking
up clean curtains.

Sukey stretched her head out of the open window, looking at the blue sky with rooks in it, looking at the delicately stirring tips of the birch-trees.

'It's time I thought of it,' she answered. 'It's only five weeks to Easter.'

Part iii

PRUDENCE came by train, and Mr Mullein met her at the station with the trap. In all her castings-up of the Halfacres forces Sukey had never reckoned in Mr Mullein as an asset. To her he seemed a dull noisy man with resounding thighs, and lips that were too red to look quite pleasant among so much, and such bristling, hair. But when she beheld him lifting down Prudence from the trap it seemed that the battle was already won, and that even Consort would have to play second fiddle, for Prudence's face was wreathed in smiles, and the gesture with which she handed Mr Mullein her umbrella reminded Sukey, in its affability, of the gesture with which Queen Victoria handed the Bible to the negro. They were both somewhat flushed, and they both smelt slightly of brandy. Mr Mullein remarked that before leaving Chelmsford he had persuaded Mrs Noman to stop at The George and take a little something to keep out the cold. Mrs Mullein did not answer. She was busy arranging the children in order of display. 'Very nice, I 'm sure,' observed Prudence as she heard their names and ages. She kept on smiling at Mr Mullein in a highly gracious and meaning manner, as if to acknowledge his skill as a father. As for Sukey, she scarcely noticed her, beyond poking her face in her direction, a poke that Sukey contrived to dodge, for it was no part of her scheme for the day to be kissed by Prudence. It was Mr Mullein who showed Prudence round the farm. It was Mr Mullein who introduced her to Consort. Leaning on his strong arm, Prudence allowed herself, with a great deal of feminine shrinking and wincing, to approach the half-door, to pat his neck, to take hold of his left horn.

'I've never set eyes on such a pair,' she said politely.

Mr Mullein blew tobacco-smoke into the bull's face. The bull bellowed and thrust against the half-door. Prudence uttered a loud whoop, and clung to her escort, who blew into the bull's face again, and then knocked out his pipe on a horn.

'By the way,' he said, as they turned back through the barton; 'I forgot to ask, how's your husband?'

They looked at each other with gleaming eyes and laughed.

When they came in Prudence instantly began praising the children, and calling them by their names. She called them all by the wrong names, and this was an opportunity for Mrs Mullein to recount their names and ages all over again, with a few ailments and peculiarities thrown in. Prudence could not believe the children to be so young. She had never seen children so advanced nor so well grown for their age. On the contrary she could not believe Consort to be so old, nor Mrs Mullein either. She was in a most polite state of disbelief. In the ailments, however, she showed a sympathetic faith, and told how her mother had cured many stubborn cases of whooping-cough by the remedy of a mouse dipped in batter, fried alive, and eaten hot before going to bed. Presently the conversation turned to deaths. Mrs Mullein recounted a few of her favourites, and then said politely :

' I saw in the paper that there has been a sad death in your part of the world.'

Seeing that Prudence looked nonplussed, she continued :

' The parson at Southend, I mean. Took ill after his own sermon, so it said, and lapsed with a clot the day after. Those clots are nasty things, wherever you have them. His was on the brain, so I understand.'

Prudence suddenly turned about.

' Why, good Lord, Suke, blessed if I hadn't nearly gone and forgot to tell you the news.

And all the way I was coming in the train I was saying to myself: " Well, I 've got something as 'll make young Suke prick up her ears." But there, that 's how it is, folks get talking, and one thing leads to another, and then my mind got took off seeing these lovely children, and the bull and all. And if you hadn't happened to mention the old man dying, I daresay I 'd have gone back without as much as mentioning it. Oh thank you, Mrs Mullein, I don't know that I won't have another, since you 're so pressing.'

Once more the cut-glass sugar-bowl was passed to Prudence, and once more she helped herself as unconcernedly as if it had come from the sixpenny bazaar. But Sukey was past worldly considerations now, she had forgotten Godmother. It had been Prudence who told her that Eric was an idiot. What had Prudence to tell her now ?

She tried to pitch her voice to the proper tone of tea-table interest.

' Do go on, Prudence.'

Prudence looked her full in the face, a strange look, cool and penetrating, and yet there was an unexpected scalliwag friendliness mixed in too. Then she winked.

' Yes, indeed, Mrs Noman, do go on. There hasn't been an order for an inquest, surely ? '

'It's not the old man, Mrs Mullein. It's his wife there's been all this set-out about. Yes, it's Mrs Seaborn. You used to be precious set on Mrs Seaborn, Suke, didn't you? Many's the time you took me up if I so much as passed a remark on her. Fair took in by her, you were, and so was other folks too. Can't see why; I never set much store on her myself, mincing about in her furs and velvets, as hypocritical as the cat coming out of the larder. Well, pride goes before a fall. I tell you, that woman didn't dare show her face at the funeral!' Prudence made an abrupt pause, sat bolt upright, and stirred her tea violently.

'You don't never say——'

Prudence's eloquence burst forth again, sweeping Mrs Mullein's arsenical hopes before it.

'What's more, there is some as declares that it was no more a stroke as finished him off than teething. No! It was the shame on her behalf as broke the old fellow's heart. I can quite believe it myself. My stars! If I live to be a hundred I shan't forget that look the Princess gave her. Withering? Withering ain't the word. And coming in front of everybody like that, you'd think it would just about kill the woman. Let alone all the talk there'd been beforehand.'

'But, Prudence, I can't make it out. What talk? What Princess?'

'Well, Suke, as to the talk, I should think you could make a pretty fair guess. People don't pop out with a full-grown son all of a sudden, what nobody's ever set eyes on or heard tell of before, without other people taking notice. And if they keep him all smuggled up, like something as has to be kept dark, well, people will take notice more. It's human nature, isn't it? Well, there was talk, and there was suspicions, and there was she trying to brazen it out, and there was old Seaborn going round as touchy as if he were all over one bunion. And so things went on, some saying the boy was covered with fish scales, so that no one couldn't bear to look at him, or else like that monster they keep in Scotland—there, there, don't look so, what's the harm?—and others saying : " No, the boy was right enough, it was her, no better than she should be in times past and now it had all come back to roost." Why, the whole town talked, and they must have talked in London too, else how should the Princess get to know of it? Anyhow, know she did. I've never seen anything to equal it, it fair made my blood run cold.'

'But, Prudence, you haven't told. What Princess?'

' Why, I 'm just coming to her. I haven't got two tongues, have I ? As a matter of fact, I can't rightly say what Princess, she 's got some outlandish name I can't get on speaking terms with. But anyhow, she 's real royalty, sure enough. And she came down for the unveiling, though why anybody should want to unveil a church as has been standing there for any one to look at as wanted to for the last hundred years it passes me to explain. Restoration, it said in the list of what folk gave. Anyhow, down she came, and there was no end of a how-d' ye-do, a platform-like set up in the churchyard, covered with red stuff, and a rope to keep the ordinary ones from crowding, and soldiers and a band from Shoebury Barracks, and carriages no end, and all the gentry, and a bishop—some say there was three or four bishops, all told, and me and the Nomans. We was there early, and I got right up against the rope, where I could see everything.

' There wasn't much to see, not to begin with, but presently the band came, and started playing, and then the gentry—the real gentry what was on the platform—they came along. And among them was Mrs Seaborn, carrying a bouquet, and Mr Seaborn looking fit to sour the milk.

' And then we waited some more, and then the

bellringers set to, and the band played God Save the Queen, and every one stood up, while the Princess got out of her carriage and stepped up on to the platform. I didn't think much of her, I must say. I should have thought she'd be wearing a train and feathers, but nothing of the sort. Poor dresser, I call her. Well, she gave us a bow or two, and then Sir Henry started leading up some of them as were on the platform. And she'd give them a little nod, and pass a remark, and then it would be the next. Well, they led up Mr Seaborn, and she didn't seem to mind him. And then came Mrs Seaborn. *She* didn't wait for no leading. Up she came with her bouquet, and dropped a curtsey, she did, and made as though she'd offer the bouquet to the Princess. And then—you should have been there to see it—the Princess she gave Mrs Seaborn that look. Not at her, it wasn't. No, she just stood there with no more expression than one of those bride-cakes you see in pastry-cooks' windows, just as though Mrs Seaborn and her bouquet were a bad smell she was too well-bred to let on about. You felt that if Mrs Seaborn didn't take the hint, the Princess would have stood like that for ever, just looking. I tell you, Suke, I can't describe it, it gives me the creeps, even to think of it.'

' What did Mrs Seaborn do ? '

' Well, maybe you won't believe it, but for a minute I thought that the Princess was going to get as good as she gave. For Mrs Seaborn, she reared up from her curtsey like a snake sitting up to bite you, wavering a little, and holding her head steady, and looking back. You could have heard a pin drop. But then some of the folks on the platform began to titter, and Mrs Seaborn, she coloured up like fire, and the Princess, she half turned round, and made pretend to say something to Sir Henry, and Mrs Seaborn went back to where she come from, and stood there all the rest of the time holding on to the bouquet as though it would break. Dangerous is what she looked, dangerous. I saw Mr Seaborn confabulating with her later on, but he might as well have spoken to an image.'

' Yes, I know,' whispered Sukey.

She was thankful for the cover of Mrs Mullein's exclamations. She did not wish Prudence to see how afraid she was, too greatly afraid to speak above a whisper, too greatly afraid to cry out upon her enemy's fall. If they would leave her alone for a little she would live down her fear. That face would pass away from her mind's eye, she would grope her way out from the terror of that recollection. Of all

Prudence's story only the ending existed for her.
The rest was a story, but this, this was true, for
she had seen it herself. A Princess, a platform,
bells ringing—then, confronting her out of this
dazzle of unrealities, Mrs Seaborn's face, a fixed
lightning. She had seen it. But then those
looks had been worn in triumph—how was it
that now they were worn in defeat?

The noise was heard of Mr Mullein cleaning
himself, and presently he came in, to be given
the breakfast-cup which had been poured out
and kept covered for him, and to hear what a tale
he had missed. Nothing loth, Prudence went
through with her story again. Mr Mullein looked
at Prudence as though he would like to tease her.

'I don't see what there is to set up such an outcry about, when all's said. Suppose the Princess
did give her a look? What harm will that do
the woman? It's my opinion there's a deal too
much fuss made about these here royalties.'

'Seeing's believing, Mr Mullein. You didn't
see that look.'

'Why, Tom, you're not going to take that
woman's part, are you? To treat her own flesh
and blood so cruel—not to have a mother's feelings even though the poor boy *was* covered all
over with scales. No! She deserves all she got,
and worse.'

'But what did she get, that's what I want to know? What's there so terrible about being looked at, whatever sort of look it were? Now if the Princess had up and boxed her ears she would have had something to complain of.'

'Shsh, Tom! What a way to speak of the Royal Blood! I wonder what the Queen said when she came to hear of it.'

'Spoke her mind, I dare say.'

Prudence, domesticated by success, helped herself to another slice of cake.

'Yes, and wouldn't she have reason too, for isn't she a mother herself? The impudence of it! Suppose the Princess had taken back those flowers to Buckingham Palace? Ah, in those olden times folk have had their heads cut off for no more and no less.'

'Well, Mrs Mullein, I can tell you, even though she's kept her head, it's precious little good to her. She'll never hold it up again, she that used to hold it so high. Doesn't dare show her face, so I hear, but sits in a room with the blinds drawn down, raging and bemoaning, and carrying on something frantic.'

'More fool she!' exclaimed Mr Mullein. 'She ought to be looking for a new husband, if she's such a fine woman. A husband would do her more good than fifty Queen Victorias.'

'The Queen doesn't like widows to marry again, so I've heard say.'

Mr Mullein remarked that Queen Victoria would be the better of a second husband herself. He'd never seen a farm thrive yet where there was a widow-owner. Then leaning towards Prudence he said : 'If your husband were to die, you wouldn't wear weepers long, I'll be bound.'

'And what about me, Thomas ? So I'm to marry again too, am I?' cried his wife rather sharply.

Sukey had raised her head. She was staring fixedly at The True Secret of England's Greatness. Her mouth was a little open, her cheeks were pink, her body, leaning forward towards the picture, was inspired and motionless. She looked like some one who beholds an extremely exciting, extremely flattering vision.

Such a vision she indeed beheld. There was Queen Victoria, and there behind her were the statesmen and the courtiers, the field-marshals, bishops, pages, and ladies-in-waiting. The Bible was still in the royal hand. Only the negro was not there ; in his place, kneeling at the foot of the throne, was Sukey Bond. She had always wanted to go to court. Now she was going.

Prudence had risen to depart. Mr Mullein was driving her into Chelmsford, and Sukey

heard Mrs Mullein promising the children that
they should all go down to the gate and wave to
their daddy. Sukey jumped out of her day-
dream and began racking her brains for some
pretext whereby she could speak to Prudence
alone for one minute ; for though Prudence had
spoken at such length of Mrs Seaborn, she had
told her nothing of Eric, and learn of him she
must, even at the cost of asking Prudence. What
could she say, how could she contrive it ? While
she was coining one subterfuge after another, and
rejecting them as fast as they were coined, she
heard Prudence addressing her.

' Suke, have you still got that spotty bodice
you wore at New Easter ? Might I have a look
at it ? I want to have some sleeves made that
way, and I can't rightly remember how they
was set in.'

' Come upstairs, and I 'll show it you.'

There was no need to make any pretence of
opening the tin box. No sooner were they
within the room than Prudence cornered her between the wall and the bed, put her face very
close and whispered : ' I 've never done you a
bad turn, have I ? Leastways, I never meant to.
And I brought you a piece of news to-day worth
hearing, didn't I ? So, Suke, be a friend and
bear this in mind. If you should happen to hear

my name mentioned in this house, you 'll speak
well of me, won't you ? Because I haven't split
on you.'

It was quite incomprehensible, but clearly
there was only one answer to be made, and she
made it.

' That' s right. You 're a good-hearted girl,
you wouldn't go mischief-making, I felt sure of
that.'

She turned to the door, but Sukey stayed her.

' Prudence, how is he ? '

' He ? Who 's he ? '

' Eric.'

' Oh, he 's all right. There wasn't nothing
wrong with him that day, just one of his fits.
I 've seen him go off like that before at the sight
of blood. Now he 's with her at Southend,
being cossetted.'

' You 're sure she 's kind to him ? '

' The girl who was there—she 's left now, because of all the unpleasantness—said she treated
him like a sugar-plum. Though Lord knows
how long that will last. For if she marries again,
as Tom says, she won't want to take him along
as a wedding-present to her next. Most likely
she 'll stow him in an asylum this time, I should
think.'

Sukey nodded. Put him in an asylum, would

they ?   She would see about that.   But she must
act quickly, there was no time to waste.

' Prudence, if you hear anything, will you send
me a letter ? '

Prudence nodded swiftly.   ' I 'm going,' she
said, and left the room with no more ado.   But
on the stairs she turned back on Sukey and for
the second time that afternoon looked her full in
the face, as though she could read there something both curious and congenial.   When she
spoke it was in a tone almost of admiration.

' Fancy you being such a sly one ! '

Sukey had not considered herself a sly one,
but now she fell to thinking that perhaps Prudence was in the right of it.   Yes, she was sly,
and presently she would be slyer yet : a thought
to glory in.   So they would put him in an
asylum, would they ?—a madhouse, such as that
which the orphans drove past in brakes on their
yearly outing to Melbury Lodge, where Mrs
Lovelace, a patroness, allowed them to pick
strawberries and walk in the park.   A solitary
house with a slate roof and many chimneys :
nothing more could be seen of it, even from the
brakes, for it was surrounded by a high wall,
built of stone and topped with iron spikes.   Behind that wall, under that roof, were the lunatics,
creatures so different from their fellows that at

the thought of them congregated there the mind quickened with a peculiar excitement, almost as if they were gas and might explode. Some one had said that when the moon was at the full the sound of their howlings could be heard for miles.

She would not think of such things. There was no need to think of them : in her determination Eric was already free, bartered for a Bible, ransomed by her slyness and by the open-handed gesture of England's Queen. She stood for a moment in the doorway, holding the cloth from which she had shaken out the crumbs, and listening to the blackbirds. They sang every evening now, but to-night they sang like creatures possessed, pouring out their wild chuckling strains as though they were doomed to joy. The sun had gone down, a watery darkness streaked the landscape ; the further pastures took on a new and intenser green as their contours flattened and dissolved, and now the whole land seemed to be flowing like a river into night ; but in the eastern sky a tall cloud still kept the colour of day, rearing up its warm rotundity, superbly substantial and alive, stationed in light above a world wheeling into darkness and unreality. A marble palace, Sukey thought : she must remember to buy a new pair of gloves before she went to see the Queen.

Somewhere under that cloud sat Mrs Seaborn, fretting in a room with all the blinds drawn down, bowed beneath a royal displeasure, plucking at the air with her white hands as though she were tearing a bunch of flowers into shreds. Some one going past the house might laugh, and she would hear it. Nothing, not closed windows or drawn curtains, could keep the sound of laughter from her now; and when the church bells were pealed on Sundays she could hear the iron clappers saying ha-ha! A new parson with his family would move into the rectory, she would look into their carefully flattened faces to read how far the news of her shame had carried. She would have to go, she would be turned out like a girl dismissed from her place. And with her would go Eric, bewildered by these changes, uneasy and self-contained as an animal subjected to change. Where would they go? Prudence had not spoken of that, saying only that the new rector was not expected before Easter.

Poor Eric, pining and solitary in that darkened house, shut away from the spring, closed in a town garden with only those mournful doves to play with!—there could be no repairing his lot; for she would never be able to explain to him that, but for this, she could not have found a way to buy him out of captivity. No, though at this moment he should see the cloud, he would not see, as she did, that hand outstretched from it, holding a Bible.

She started, discovering suddenly that she was looking at a star. It was late, she must stand dreaming here no longer, forgetting her duty to the Mulleins, whom she intended so soon and so undutifully to desert. ' If I give them a week's notice, can I endure to wait so long ? ' she asked herself as she ran indoors ; and that night, listening to the rumble of the waggons along the road to London, she decided that she could not keep Eric waiting for the sake of observing such punctilios as these. She must run away from her second place as she had done from her first, leaving behind another letter of explanation. The day after to-morrow, to-morrow itself ? She settled upon the day after to-morrow. To-morrow, as a sop to conscience, should be given over to dealing thoroughly with the mending-basket. But not a patch was set, not a button replaced, and by course of one day's neglect six of the young Mulleins contrived to annihilate every semblance of having been properly looked after for months. That evening there could have been no hearing the blackbirds, even had she had time to listen for them. The air rang with laughter and hallooings and with quacks of

rage and frustration ; for the children had put
into practice a game recommended to them by
Prudence : to bait either end of a piece of string
with a gobbet from the pigpail and to throw it
among the ducks. Indoors Sukey sat nursing
the baby, who choked and wailed, while Mrs
Mullein said over and over again : ' It 's that
diptheria, I know it is. Why doesn't he come ? '

Both ducks and Mulleins had been herded to
their rest before the doctor arrived. He carried
the child to the lamp. Fractious with pain and
sleepiness, it yelled as he prised open its jaws.
After looking down its throat for a moment he
said gravely : ' Can you give me a crochet-hook ? '
—and the crochet-hook being found by Sukey
he drew out a slobbered tangle of darning-wool.
There was no vestige of a grin on his weary face
as he left the room, but two days later, when
Sukey opened the door to him again, he greeted
her with a wink so well modulated that it seemed
as though he had been perfecting it ever since
their last meeting. This time, however, he came
for a more serious matter. Mrs Mullein had
been so much upset by the baby's misadventure
that on the following day she spilled a panful of
boiling fat over her foot, and as the doctor was
only summoned for the children the neglected
scald had got into a bad way before she gave in

and took to her bed. Now, he said, it must be a matter of ten days before she could get about again.

' O Sukey, what a blessing it is you 're here to see to Mullein and the children ! ' wailed the invalid. Sukey nodded, and tried to view affairs in the same light.

She had no doubts as to her ability to see to the children, but in regard to Mullein she was not quite so sure. Seeing to a man, she considered, meant cooking him three meat meals a day and watching him while he ate them. Further, she suspected that it included a discreet amount of keeping him up to his work. She was not able to carry out either of these obligations as she could have wished, as her charge was now scarcely ever at home to be practised upon. Appearing half-way through the morning in a collar, he would put the horse into the trap and drive off, saying that he was off to look at some new stock, or that he must go into Chelmsford to see about the mortgage. ' Will you be back to dinner ? ' He would nod ; and then, just as he rounded the gate, he would look back over his shoulder and shout : ' No ! '

Sometimes on these afternoons, if she had time, Sukey would take two or three of the younger children and walk round the farmlands.

Ignorant as she was, she knew enough of farming by now to see that much needed doing, and that in Mr Mullein's absence little was done. Since the snowfall the weather had been dry, with a parching east wind, and except in the brook meadows there was no grass feed for the beasts. Yet twice she found the complaining ewes turning over and over the gnawed-out mangold tops, and walking petulantly away when their lambs tried to suck, and another time she came on a bullock lying down, motionless, dead. Its mouth was open, there was blood on its gums where it had scratched itself, trying to stay its hunger by biting at the hedge. Its happier companions had broken fence, and were in the next field, ravenously destroying a haystack.

That evening Mr Mullein was later than ever. 'Whatever can have come to Mullein?' his wife repeated, varying the inquiry with: 'Whatever can be the matter with Consort?' At length the bellowing ceased, and remembering that bullock Sukey was struck with a fear. As she crossed the barton she heard a rasping sound: the noise of Consort's tongue writhing and searching over a metal surface. The cowman had forgotten to water him. The cowman lived in the village, he was enjoying his supper half a mile away. Sukey strained her ears for the clop-

clop of Mr Mullein's horse, but there was nothing
to be heard but the chatter of the brook and
Consort's licking tongue.   She filled a bucket at
the well, unbarred the door and went into the
shed.   As she set down the bucket the bull
swung his head towards her, loomed up beside
her and began to drink.   Clumsy with haste he
upset the bucket and fell to licking the spilled
water from the ground.   She took up the bucket
and went out to fill it for the second time.   When
she turned from the well the bull was standing
beside her.   In the dusk he was enormous, and
his bulk seemed to blot out what light there was
left in the dim air.   He snuffed, and lowered his
head towards the water.   Stepping warily over
the uneven ground she walked back into the
darkness of the shed with the bull's darkness
following at her heels.   This time she remembered to bar the door.   She began to tremble,
but it seemed to her that she was trembling not
so much with fear as with awe.   By the time she
had got back into the house she was trembling
with plain downright anger, and when Mr Mullein
had returned and eaten his supper she let fly and
spoke her mind, and found much satisfaction in
doing so.   She was growing up fast now ; she
could scold like a woman.

Yes, Mr Mullein was a bad farmer, and Mrs

Mullein was a bad healer. ' I will give notice on quarter-day,' she said to herself ; but on quarter-day Mrs Mullein was still a-bed, and it was almost with hatred in her heart that she found herself looking at the first primroses. One day there were two or three, the next day there were thousands, for the drought had broken at last, and the thirsty dust in the lane smelt like summer. Alice came clattering into the kitchen with the news that they must all gather primroses for the Easter decorations, schoolmistress had said so. ' And I know where I shall pick mine, but nobody else is to know, or they will all be gone before Good Friday.' At the orphanage Good Friday had been most religiously observed with a dinner of salt cod and Miss Pocock prostrated with a sick headache, but now Sukey was expected to cut jam sandwiches, fill a bottle with weak tea, and set out with the children, carrying a hank of darning-wool, and also a clasp-knife in case they found any well-bloomed sprays of palm. All the young people of the village were out primrosing. Two adders were seen, Rosie Gibson climbed a tree and could not get down again until her young man climbed up after her. The tree swayed and quivered, and every one stood underneath exclaiming that it would certainly break. ' Are those your Easter garters,

Rosie ? ' ' O you saucebox ! You just wait till I 'm down again.'

William Cowley came and tumbled a capful of primroses into Sukey's lap as she sat at the edge of the copse with little Louise beside her on her spread-out skirts.

' What 's the matter with her ? ' he asked. ' Why doesn't she go picking along of her sisters ? '

' She 's stung herself on the nettles, and thought it was a snake.'

' Lucky for her it weren't. Kitty Pring nearly put her hand on one, only she heard it hiss. Did you ever see a snake ? '

She nodded.

He stood for a while beside her, watching her hands that gathered the primrose knots, and finished off each knot with a frill of leaves, and wound the pinkish wool round the pink stalks. Afterwards she wished that he had stayed to sit down by her and talk, for on this gay afternoon it seemed incomplete to have no other company than her own thoughts and a sneezing child who didn't belong to her ; but at the time she had scarcely noticed that he had moved away, for his words had called up other words in her mind. ' Like a snake sitting up to bite you,' Prudence had said. And Eric was still moping in Southend, the prisoner of a mother who might marry again and send him to an asylum. They would be moving out soon. Where would they go, why had there been no letter from Prudence? And why had she been silly enough to place any faith in Prudence's help? When, when would Mrs Mullein's leg relent, and heal, and set her free to go to London?

On Easter morning she was roused by the strains of a hymn.

'Jesus Christ is risen to-day-ay!' sang Mrs Mullein, still in bed. Sukey turned over, bit her pillow, and shook with hysterical laughter.

Three days before, being carried away by the general glorification of a country Holy Week, she had prepared an iced cake to greet the Risen Lord, a cake trimmed with a yellow cotton-wool duckling, a wreath of sugar daisies, and the word Alleluia on a pink scroll. It was indeed a very fine cake; but as she fetched it from the larder and placed it on the glass cake-stand in the centre of the table it seemed to her a mockery. Christ rising, the ducklings breaking from their shells, the short-stemmed childish daisies poking up from the greensward—all were escaping, had escaped; she stayed in prison and designed cakes which would be eaten but never admired. As for the cotton-wool duckling, she had been a fool to spend twopence on him, since the children would quarrel to possess him, snatch and crumple him, then leave him to grow dusty, to become litter, to be swept up with crumbs and cinders; and that would be his end. She set down the cake-stand with a bang and flounced out of the room; for Mrs Mullein was calling her again.

'Go to the front door, Sukey. I've seen a trap turn in at the gate. And wait a minute, girl. Just hand me the lavender water in case it's gentry calling.'

'As if they couldn't knock for themselves,' said Sukey under her breath as she ran downstairs. 'Knock they shall, too. I've got the tea to set, and the kettle on the boil, and not one of those children with clean hands. Yes, knock away. How many legs do you suppose a girl has?'

'Sukey! Sukey! Can't you hear the door?'

The front door was seldom used, and stuck in wet weather. She wrenched it open, and just contrived to stay herself from exclaiming: 'Why, you're the apple-woman!'

At the same moment two of the children charged down the passage crying out: 'It's Godmother!' And immediately the resemblance was gone for ever, and Sukey saw only an oldish

lady, rather tall and rather stout, wearing a
mackintosh cape and shaking the rain from a
large umbrella, and having all about her, just
as the linen-cupboard, the copper kettle, and the
tea-caddy had, the air of being certain to last for
a long time and repay polishing, the air of being
Good.

Sukey held out her hands for the mackintosh
cape and the umbrella. She knew at sight that
this was not the kind of woman to carry wet
clothes into a dry house. As she stood waiting
she praised God inwardly that the teapot was
still in the back kitchen and so eligible for a good
rub-up. The children were none of them as she
could have wished them to be, and it was impossible to keep Mrs Mullein tidy in bed, she
was not that sort; but she did not think that
Godmother would find much to complain of
about the chairs or the table.

Mrs Disbrowe—that was Godmother's name
—made no comments of any kind when she
came downstairs from Mrs Mullein's bedroom
and drew up for tea. She made a very good
meal, sitting her chair as such chairs should be
sat: squarely and uprightly, with her elbows
well down and a pocket handkerchief disposed
upon her knees.

'And what do you think of Emma's leg?'

inquired Mr Mullein. 'Speaking for myself, I've never seen a leg look angrier.'

'Yes, 'tis a bad leg,' replied she composedly.

'Three bottles of lotion and a pot and a half of ointment she's used already, no less. And yet it don't mend.'

'That's one of the comforts of doctor's stuff,' observed Mrs Disbrowe. 'You can count the bottles.'

There was a pause, broken by Mr Mullein exclaiming 'Bottles,' in a voice that suggested a desire to be playful. Presently he said 'Bottles' once more, and completed the innuendo by imitating the sound of a cork being drawn. The children laughed. Mrs Disbrowe turned her calm gaze towards him, politely attentive to the sally of wit he laboured with.

'There's better things in bottles than doctor's stuff, eh, Mrs Disbrowe?'

'Certainly there be.'

It had occurred to Sukey that Mr Mullein was not wholly at his ease in Godmother's company, and that Godmother herself was aware of this, and viewed his galvanic fawnings with something like complacence. Mr Mullein, however, felt himself encouraged, and set about another repartee, tilting back his chair to give himself confidence.

' How 's the Duke ? '

The sugar fell into Mrs Disbrowe's second cup with a loud plop, such was Sukey's surprise. Mr Mullein turned to her, invigorated. She was small game, but she was better than nothing.

' You wasn't expecting to hear us naming dukes, was you ? P'raps I 'd better introduce you. Miss Sukey Bond, the Duchess of Kent. Duchess of Kent, Miss Sukey Bond. Sukey, the Duchess will trouble you for another slice of cake.'

Mr Mullein laughed very loud and the children tee-hee'd.

' I keep a public called The Duke of Kent. It 's that which Mr Mullein was inquiring after.'

' Yes,' guffawed Mr Mullein. ' And that 's why I calls her the Duchess. I always do.'

The Duke of Kent. The Duchess of Kent. Queen Victoria was their child, rather surprisingly, since how should a duchess, wearing only feathers, bring forth a crowned Queen ? Sukey glanced towards The True Secret of England's Greatness, and then towards Mrs Disbrowe, and then back to The True Secret again. The True Secret had come to Halfacres from Godmother. Perhaps all publics called The Duke of Kent were obliged by the law of England loyally to possess a picture of his illustrious child. Per-

haps such pictures were served out yearly by the
Government, like the postman's new coat, and
that was why Mrs Disbrowe had been in a position to give this one away. These suppositions
made Mrs Disbrowe appear very splendidly in
Sukey's eyes, almost as though she were one of
The Family.

While Sukey was washing up the tea-things
Mrs Disbrowe came into the back kitchen and
took her umbrella from the bucket where it had
been set to drain. Then she put on her cape,
picked up a basket and walked to the door. It
was still raining, the camomile tufts in the yard
were silvered with a fine web of moisture. Mrs
Disbrowe glanced down at her boots.

'I'm old-fashioned,' she said. 'Is there such
a thing as a pair of pattens in this house?'

Remembering to have seen such hanging up in
the woodhouse, Sukey fetched them, and knelt at
Mrs Disbrowe's feet to fasten them on. She was
going back to the sink when Mrs Disbrowe said:

'Put on your outdoor things and come with
me.'

They walked in silence through the yard into
the pasture. Mounted upon her pattens Mrs
Disbrowe moved with the stature of a goddess.
Sukey felt that conversation would be out of the
question with one so far above her, whose grey

eyes must see so much further afield than hers could do. It was peaceful to be out of doors and cooled with the fine rain after a whole day spent in human concerns—in praising God and finding the places in the prayer-book for the little Mulleins all gaping after their primroses, or in ministering to the kitchen range and the sink. With every step she felt herself walking into a larger area of time, time ordered and disposed, wherein there was room for all things, all creatures, to grow and manifest themselves and be fulfilled; room even for Eric and herself to meet once more and delight noiselessly in love, like the plants around her standing mute in the warm spring rain. She tilted up her face to feel the rain on her eyelids, and suddenly was conscious of a blackbird singing near by, in the little birch-wood. It seemed to her that he was saying : ' Eric, Eric, Eric,' and then on a lower note : ' Sukey.'

Mrs Disbrowe stopped, and pointed to a rosette of lined and rather fleshy leaves.

' Do you know what those are ? '

' Plantains, ma'am.'

' Fill this basket with them for me. Only the young leaves, mind. The plump ones. And don't hurry.'

While Sukey roamed through the fields, choosing plantain leaves and getting her feet very agreeably wet and experiencing all the pleasantly important sensations of a child deputed to do something grown-up and responsible, Mrs Disbrowe, stately upon her pattens, remote under the dome of her umbrella, remained by the hedgerow, surveying the landscape and watched attentively by some cows. And when the basket was filled to her approval, and they turned back to the farm, these cows with one accord swung round and followed her.

That night, in her first sleep, Sukey dreamed that she was going with Mrs Disbrowe to see the Queen. Mrs Disbrowe was partly the Duchess of Kent, she wore the signboard of her inn round her neck like a locket, and carried in her hand a quantity of black ostrich feathers. After walking through London streets they came to the door of the Queen's palace. Here Mrs Disbrowe stopped. 'You must go in alone,' she said. Immediately Sukey found herself in an upper room of the palace; and yet, after the way of dreams, she knew that much time had passed. She looked from a window and saw Mrs Disbrowe standing where she had left her, standing patient and superb as she had stood in the pasture. Around her the houses of London had dwindled so that they rose no higher than her knees, and grass was growing from the pavement. An impressive dream, as Mrs Disbrowe was an impressive woman; though, when one came to think it over, somewhat uncommunicative, as was she. For now, looking back on the events of the day, Sukey for the first time remembered that none of those expected comments on the good estate of the linen-cupboard, tea-caddy, etc., had been made: Godmother had shown no more housewifely concern than the veriest gipsy or the veriest Queen. 'But she did take notice, I vow,' murmured Sukey, settling herself anew in trustfulness and repose. She felt absolute confidence in that decoction of plantain.

The confidence was justified. On the morrow Mrs Mullein's leg had already begun to cleanse itself and to heal, and on the doctor's next visit he declared himself perfectly satisfied with the result of his treatment and spoke of the conquests of modern medicine. Mrs Mullein had been downstairs for two days, and Sukey was word-perfect in the act of giving notice, when Mr Mullein was gored to death by the bull.

Consort had long borne him a grudge, the cowman said; and Lydia and Fanny, who had come to wash and lay out the corpse, nodded their heads consentingly, and whispered that if Consort had indeed hated his owner, he had

glutted himself with revenge. 'Bruised? Tore?'
—Rhoda seemed almost to chant the words.
'His body was like a puddle.' Within doors
Mrs Mullein wept and wailed, and gathered her
children about her, and declared that she was
going to America. To all who came to condole
with her, and to the undertaker, and to the estate
agent, she told the same tale; and when the
Reverend Mulberry Glossop spoke of Mr Mullein's departure to a Better Land, she asked him
if he had ever known any one who had been
blown up in a Mississippi steamboat. Pity was
wasted upon a person so obviously enjoying
herself.

'Have you written to Mrs Disbrowe?
Wouldn't you like her to be with you for the
funeral?'

'Godmother never goes to funerals. She
don't hold with the clergy. I wonder if she'd
let me have that yellow trunk?'

Mr Mullein had not been underground two
hours when Sukey was sent into Chelmsford with
a shopping list of articles for America. It was
a long walk, and the shopping took some time;
dusk was falling when she carried the larger
parcels to the carrier's office, whence they would
be brought to Halfacres on the following day.
The carrier's office was in the Square, next to The

George Hotel, and as she left it Sukey had the feeling that she was being stared at. She looked round : there was no one in the street that she knew, and she was about to walk on again when she saw Prudence, looking out on her from behind the fern and the looped lace curtains of the George parlour. Sukey smiled and nodded, and had half a mind to stop for a word with Prudence and the chance, maybe, of some news of Eric ; but even as she hesitated, and half turned back, Prudence drew away from the window with a furious unrecognising glare. Prudence in one of her tempers again : perhaps she was fancying herself that Princess.

She had been trudging for a good half-hour through the silence and earthy dusk of the lanes when she heard footsteps coming swiftly up behind her. Once or twice before, she had fancied that she was being followed, and had glanced back, perturbed, thinking of gipsies, and clutching tighter Mrs Mullein's purse ; but the lane had curved behind her, as it curved before her, unpeopled. The thought of being followed was not made any pleasanter by thinking that the pursuer was keeping out of sight, and it was with a kind of relief that she heard the footsteps gaining on her, and knew that the pursuer had come into the open.

'Stop!'

The voice was hoarse and breathless.

'Stop, I say. Whatever's come over you, Sukey Bond, that you won't stop?'

It was Prudence. Prudence was dressed in her grandest apparel, but her bonnet was tilted over one eye, her skirts were splashed with mud, and her hand, in a tight kid glove, was clenched about a tattered hazel-twig, seemingly torn out of the hedge at random. Her face was pale and set, her body twitched as though she were sobbing inwardly, her eyes were so bright that they seemed to stab the dusk. Sukey's first thought was, that she was drunk; but she was too sharp and pale for drunkenness: perhaps she had gone out of her mind.

'Why, Prudence, what a surprise to see you here! Is anything the matter? Are you upset?'

Prudence did not seem to have heard. Her eyes stabbed quite blindly into the dusk, and the silly lamb's tails on the hazel-twig jerked to and fro with the tremor of her body. Suddenly she ejaculated:

'Are you still at Halfacres?'

'Yes.'

'Oh! You are, are you?'

There was another pause. Then, as though she had tautened all the energies of her body for this one act, Prudence ripped off the lamb's tails from the hazel-twig.

'Well, you can take a message there from me. You can tell Mr Mullein with Mrs Noman's compliments that I 've better things to do than to sit all day in the George parlour, waiting for a man that 's tied to his wife's apron-strings, and hasn't got no more spunk than a louse. And you can tell him that I 've waited once, and I won't wait again and that he needn't think to whistle me back, for if it were his dying breath, I wouldn't come. And you can tell him that I 've paid for the drinks, and that he need never think of me no more, and that I 'm done with men and their ways henceforward, for I 'm not one to be made a fool of twice. And that seemingly he doesn't know the difference between a flesh-and-blood woman and a sopped dishclout, so that he 'd better be a faithful husband in future, since it 's all one to him, so he can keep to his lawful dishclout, tell him. And I wish him joy of her, that 's all. You can tell him all this, with my compliments, and if so be she 's there, tell on. I 'd as lief she heard it as not. That 's all. Now I 'm going.'

Sukey ran after her.

'O Prudence, you don't know what you 're saying.'

'Yes, I do.'

'No! No, you don't. Prudence, Prudence, take it back!'

'Take it back?' Prudence turned about. 'I won't take back a word of it. Here! I 've thought of something else. Tell him I 'll remember him in my prayers along with his bull.'

'Hush, hush!'

Sukey was trembling. Prudence surveyed her sharply and seized hold of her.

'You creeping little whore, do you mean to say you are after him too?'

'Prudence, for heaven's sake, don't utter another word. Him you 're speaking of—he 's dead.'

That night, sitting on the earthy floor of the waggon, huddled for warmth among the green sheaves of mint and sage, Sukey thought of all the people in the Bible who had run away from their places at God's bidding: the Israelites led by Moses and Aaron and Miriam—it was a good thing that a responsible woman was one of that party, to see to the provisions and the hundred and one oddments that men have no patience for—Lot, Joseph warned by a dream, Paul and Silas, and Master Christian too, almost a Bible character. There was a heartening number of them, and all most respectable characters: if justification were needed, she was running away

in good company. But justification was not
needed : God showed His sign, sent His angel,
sounded His trump—one had no choice before
that bidding, one ran away as one was bid. In
the lane between Chelmsford and Halfacres God
had showed His sign, had brandished before her
the appalling nature of love. This love was not
a thing to be trifled with, or to be weighed
against duties, or to be put off with a pretext,
with a *presently* : one might not request it to
dance attendance on a bad leg, to cool its ruthless heels until a funeral had been tidied away
and a trunk packed. Looking at love in the lane
between Chelmsford and Halfacres, Sukey had
seen all her scruples and vanities of obligation
vanish like a handful of dust thrown in at the
open door of a furnace. Even while she strove
to stay Prudence's outburst of rage she had felt
her inmost being cry out in a kind of triumph :
'This is how I, too, love !'—and afterwards, with
a more magnificent and sombre boast : ' This is
how I should be, if I were to lose him.' The
sense of being a fellow-initiate had made it impossible for her to feel much pity for Prudence :
one does not pity one's equals, the soldier feels
no special compassion for the comrade who falls
beside him, compassion is stretched out over the
whole battlefield and with a haughty excitement

embraces all—an old harrow, the shells flying through the air, the look of a thistle spattered with blood. Having seen Prudence depart, moving like a woman made of dead clay, she had picked up her parcels and walked on briskly with all her thoughts running before her like obedient servants, with this to decide and that to do to make ready for her departure.

For she was going to London to see the Queen ; and she was going at once, that very night. Too much time had been wasted already— precious time, hours and hours of Eric's freedom and happiness, cast to the Mulleins. How long was it since Prudence had come to Halfacres with her tale of the Princess ? Five weeks, six weeks ?—long enough anyhow for her to love her Tom Mullein, and have him and lose him. Long enough, horribly long enough while she had been dawdling here, for Eric to be lost to her ; and it was with agony that she heard the screech of the whistle, and saw the smoke bulge along the embankment, and knew that though she had money enough to buy a ticket she would not be able to go by train to London that day. But biddable and competent, a thought raced forward to the end of the Halfacres lane, to the London road where the waggons bound for Covent Garden rumbled by. So she had reached the farm, and performed her evening tasks and said good-night and gone up to her attic ; and there, dealing stealthily lest she should wake the children, had packed her belongings, and made sure of the money in her purse, and put on her Sunday clothes, and lowering herself cautiously down the creaking stairs had let herself out of the house, acting coolly, securely, almost thought-lessly, always moved forward by the one strong compulsion. And so, seated on her box at the lane end, motionless and still travelling stead-fastly on through time, she had waited for the sound of wheels.

It was the glow of the waggon lantern, dwell-ing intermittently upon the darkness, which first answered her expectation ; the sound of wheels came after, tunnelling its way through the silence. In the bank opposite two vivid unwinking sparks glowed : the eyes of a poaching cat ; and immediately she saw her shadow flow out upon the hedge and the waggon came round the corner.

' Do you go to London ? '

He checked his horse. A soft swishing and rustling was heard, as the sheafed herbs in the waggon brushed against each other.

' May I ride with you ? '

He answered her in a sleepy voice, and showed

small curiosity or surprise. She received the impression that she was to him little more than some creature of the night, a moth or a dream ; something that would have no daylight validity, no power to remain in his waking thoughts. But he was kind in an unconcerned way : lent her a hand with the box, hollowed out a small burrow for her among the herbs—for she would be warmer there at the back, he said—and gave her an empty sack to sit on, and another to put over her knees.

A lantern hung from the shaft. When the wheels jolted over a rut or a stone it widened its swing and cast a sudden hoary being upon the trees that overhung the roadway. An owl hooted. A shooting star traversed the sky. A rabbit squealed in the hedge. Once they passed a gipsy encampment in a clearing. The caravan was all sealed up, a boxful of strange slumbers, but the fire still winked a drowsy ember or two, and lit up a battered corned-beef tin and an old broom. The dog barked, straining at the rope which tethered him. Further on they passed a farm, and there the house-dog barked, and woke a flotilla of ducks on the pond. They swam up and down, quacking wildly, and the waters of the pond lollopped softly against the soft mud.

Tilth and pasture, an orchard, the smell of

cows, a rickyard, a cock crowing and other cocks replying, trees and more trees, sometimes the mouth of a lane with a sign-post pointing into darkness, a milestone, a farmstead and the smell of dung, a clanking water-vane, a toll-house, and more trees, and another milestone; a flock of sheep huddled on a rise of ground, a high park wall and a pair of stone gate-posts, and another milestone and more trees; a market garden, and a row of new cottages, and a little town with a lighted window here and there and cats strolling about the street; then tilth and pasture again, and the gurgle of running water, and mist filling up a hollow; and another farmstead and more trees.

Trees. Mysterious creatures that stay out all night.

By day they have the character we give them, submitting themselves to names and usage. The wheelwright walks among them and sees in the living limb a shaft or an axle-tree; the woodman marks one for destruction, another for continuance, and the old women creep into the copse for a faggot; the farmer drives his pigs under the oak and finds the patriot there. They are all known by their kind—the fruitful apple-tree, the treacherous elm that on a windless summer afternoon will cast off a dead bough like a garment and kill an old gentleman watching a cricket match. But at night they regain themselves and become trees once more, assuming their full stature, their proper amazing shape—the trunk rising from the ground with the energy of a torrent, sweeping up to the release of boughs, arms too proud to seek after anything but air. Then even the humblest old apple-tree with a clothes-line fastened to it escapes from its drudgery into an arboreal aloofness, and the elms which have been by day mere incidents in the hedgerow stand up against the sky like a race of giants. They give back the wind buffet for buffet, or hang above the meadow more heavily than a thunder-cloud. The traveller sees them far off, and approaches them with a kind of fear, awed by that rooted bulk awaiting his puny transit, half persuaded that he may distinguish in that overhead muttering the articulation of an ancient spite, an ancient scorn.

Now the moon, an old unwilling moon, had risen, and showed the landscape all confused with the mist, silently boiling up from every hollow. I am not really afraid, thought Sukey. It is the night. But she shut her eyes, resolving that she would not open them until her mind's eye had quite forgotten how like a wolf a tree could look, and breathed up the smell of the herbs all round her. They had a comforting smell of earth and cookery. It is only the night, she thought again. Trees are really quite kind. And she began to recall, one by one, the trees she had known : the little birch-wood bowed under its clanking winter fruits, the ilexes in the Dannie churchyard, the pear-tree under which she had sat with Eric, the limes by the rectory stable-yard, the monkey-puzzle at the orphanage—this last a trifle austere and dusty, perhaps, but quite good at heart, and wearing with the utmost patience a foliage so enduring and unbecoming that one might suppose it had been contracted for, along with the other uniforms. Now she was going back to London. How striking it would be if the road to Covent Garden should pass the orphanage ! The thought darted into her mind that by night London could be seen far off, a red portending glow upon the sky. She peeped round to see if the waggoner's back was outlined by this phenomenon, but he sat as before, shown off by nothing more remarkable than a few stars. She must be patient, and wait for some more milestones before she looked again. Another milestone, and more trees ; but the trees were not wolfish now—that one, with its trunk all newly feathered out, was like a cochin-china fowl. A row of new cottages, and a

market-garden with the glass frames shining in
the moonlight, and an inn with a signboard
hanging from an ash-bough, and more market-
gardens.   They must surely be nearing London;
it would soon be time to look round for that
glow.   But she did not move.   Her limbs were
heavy, and the chill of overlong waking sent
her burrowing further in among the herbs.

She awoke with a start.   The waggon had
stopped; it was light, and the mint-leaves tickling
her nose were green, and through them she saw
houses.   The narrow street was crowded with
waggons, and there was a great noise of men
shouting and horses trampling the cobbles, and
a delicious smell of fruit hung in the air.   Quantities of pigeons ran along the roof gutters or
swooped down among the waggon-wheels.
In the light of dawn London seemed a mottle
of pigeon's-breast colours—brown and plum-
coloured brick, and the different greys of slate
and lead and streaked stone.   A hundred church
clocks began to tell the hour, and a sweep
appeared round the corner.

There was a clamour of gee-upping and whip-
cracking, and slowly, with many stops and
delays, the procession of waggons made its way
into the market.   Sukey's driver jumped down,
came round to the back of the waggon and began

taking down the tail-board. He caught sight of Sukey among the herbs, and started with surprise.

'Blessed if I hadn't forgotten all about you. You're a bit stiff, I reckon. Here, catch hold of me and I'll jump you down. Friends meeting you?'

'They're not expecting me yet,' she answered.

Sukey had not foreseen very accurately what steps she must take between Covent Garden and Buckingham Palace. In no case could she, with any good manners, burst in upon the Queen before breakfast. She supposed that a queen would not take breakfast much before half-past eight—there were several hours which she could give to a consideration of what to do next, and Covent Garden Market seemed as good a place as any other to consider in: it had this merit, at any rate, that she knew where she was.

'Would there be any objection to me sitting here for a while?' she asked.

'Don't suppose so,' said he. 'Provided you don't get in any one's way, or get yourself moved on by the police.'

He looked at her a little dubiously while she settled herself upon her box; then whistled, and walked back to his waggon.

Sukey prepared herself for consideration. Presently she began to doubt if Covent Garden

Market was really a very suitable spot to consider in ; there was so much going on, and so many exciting things to look at. She decided to consider with her eyes shut. By now the sun had risen, and the newly warmed air was a caress to her limbs. She discovered that instead of considering she had fallen asleep.

Perhaps after all I will not consider, she concluded. I will just think. The best ideas often come into one's head while one is just thinking. Having agreed on this with her conscience, Sukey was perfectly at liberty to observe as much as she pleased.

The market was much fuller now. Buyers walked among the sellers, the porters were beginning to carry away purchases, and the costers and flower-women were holding an auction among themselves in one corner. Besides these workaday folk Sukey saw with bewilderment a quantity of gentry, all youthful, grand and gay, and dressed as though for a ball. In a proper gentry manner they did not appear to be doing anything except enjoy themselves, gazing and exclaiming, and seeming perfectly at home. One lady, with the smallest feet that Sukey had ever beheld, was very systematically feeding the costers' donkeys with carrots, and a young gentleman, holding more carrots, walked behind her, with a second, more full-blown and larger-footed lady leaning on his arm. His expression was a little useful; yet he too must clearly be enjoying himself—else why should he be there at all? It was all very mysterious and surprising, and Sukey was at a loss to account for it until there flashed upon her a recollection of the orphans' yearly outing among Mrs Lovelace's strawberry beds. No doubt the gentry had outings too; and just as it was a rarity for the orphans to stay up late so would it be a rarity for the gentry to get up early. Meanwhile the buyers and sellers went on with their business, and paid no more attention to these visitors than to the pigeons.

Being still rather sleepy and already so much surprised, she was able to take it fairly quietly when, the crowd parting, she saw a blue dog. Perhaps the gentry preferred their dogs blue. However, she was sufficiently aroused to wish to see the dog again and watched closely for another glimpse of it. The market was now at its busiest, and she seemed likely to lose her pains. Conscience struck in, observing that she was here, not to gape after strange dogs, but to consider soberly and maturely how best to make her way into Buckingham Palace. Was she by now sufficiently wakeful to be able to close her eyes? Besides, the dog could not have been blue;

such a thing was against nature. Most likely it was a grey dog. She had only seen it for an instant, and one's eyes will play one strange tricks.

But at that moment the dog was disclosed once more, quite unmistakably blue—as blue as wood-smoke. It was a large dog, and furry, with a mane like a lion and small erect ears. It paid not the smallest attention to the jostle of the market, appearing to have come there, like Sukey, for the purposes of meditation : Only, it is much better at it than me, she thought. At last her curiosity and a respectful fellow-feeling made her rise and approach it. 'Poor fellow,' she said, and felt the inadequacy of the speech. Its brow was covered with a most inviting plush, and plush gaitered its fore-paws ; she could no longer withstand the temptation to saunter her palm over that voluptuous surface. She put out her hand, she had almost attained her wish when the dog, slightly rousing from its hermitage of fur and abstraction, gave her a look. She retreated, not in fear, but as one retreats from a shrine. She was delaying for one last glance when she saw it prick its ears and stir the tip of its tail. Its attention was directed upon a building called *Coffee-House*, a spirited coffee-house where trade was in full swing, for wafts of voices and the smell of bacon issued thence, and behind the geraniums in the window-boxes waiters could be seen whisking to and fro. The blue dog rose to its feet briskly, and as though worked by a spring its tail curled over its back and began to wag. Flattening its ears it advanced to meet a gentleman who came out of the coffee-house, dressed, as the other gentry had been, for a ball. He put out a very white hand and pinched its ear. The dog stretched itself, and yawned, a little reproachfully.

Sukey could not restrain herself. She cried out:

'Why, it's got a blue tongue!'

Her astonishment had made her speak loudly. The dog's gentleman turned round, looked at her, smiled; he made a step towards her, then thought better of it and walked away.

She went back to her box and sat down again, suddenly dispirited. It would have been pleasant to have a word with somebody. She would have liked to stroke that dog. A gentleman rich enough to own a blue dog might impart some valuable advice on how to behave with royalty. But of course one should never allow oneself to get into conversation with strangers; and of course one should remember one's place. She shut her eyes with energy and forced herself into consideration.

She was still considering when, about a quarter of an hour later, a smell, familiar and ineffably comforting, made her look up. The dog's gentleman was standing beside her with a cup and saucer in either hand.

' Won't you have a cup of tea ? '

Though she was too confused to speak, at any rate she could rise, remembering her place. But he stayed her.

' Don't. You 'll only spill it. These cups slide about so.'

If only he would sit down too ! But then in this rude place there was nothing for him to sit on. Blushing deeply and too much aware of her place to look higher, she shot a grateful glance towards the gentleman's trousers. The gentry always stood like that : on one leg, as though they were allied to flowers.

' A cup of tea is always pleasant, don't you think ? '

' It is indeed. And this is such lovely tea, too. So strong ! '

He poured some into the saucer and set it down by the dog, who sniffed at it, looked hurt, and turned his back.

' Indian tea,' observed the gentleman thoughtfully.

There was a pause, during which Sukey debated if good manners would now oblige her to make some remark about India. From India one might lead the conversation round to the Crown Jewels, from the Crown Jewels—the clocks began to chime again, the pigeons to whirr out of the belfries. Sukey put down her teacup, clenched her hands together, drew a long breath, and said :

'If you please, sir, can you tell me how I can get to Buckingham Palace ? '

He began to give her directions, embroiling himself in the attempt to be perfectly explicit. She forgot her shyness, and looked him in the face, her whole soul intent on his words.

' And there it is, straight in front of you.' He ended abruptly, as though he had lost the thread of what he was saying.

The words seemed to sweep her forward, to leave her standing alone before a reality. This Buckingham Palace, then, to her a word and a dream, existed, and was close at hand ; and others knew it, and vouched for it, and took it for granted as a thing seen day by day.

She said in a low voice : ' Is it very large ? '

' It is very large,' he answered, watching her face. ' It is built of stone, and in front of it there are tall iron railings, and iron gates. And by the gate there stands a sentry with a fixed bayonet, on guard.'

He was silent, still watching her. Then suddenly he pulled forward an empty hamper, turned it upside down and sat down at her side.

'Tell me—I know I have no right to ask questions—but please tell me why you want to go to Buckingham Palace ? Do you want to see the Queen ?'

'If you please, sir, yes.'

Now that he was sitting down, and had begun to ask sensible questions, it was easy to forget that he was a gentleman—the only gentleman she had ever spoken to except Mr Warburton—and to think only that he was a little like Eric ; for he spoke softly, and moved limberly, and had, as Eric had, an air of being only lightly tethered to reality. This last quality was especially reassuring to her. It would not have been easy to explain her intentions to any one very practical. To him, asking about the journey and if she had not felt the cold, it seemed to be enough that she *had* intentions ; and she was grateful to him for not pressing her as to the reasons which made it so imperative that she should see the Queen. When he went away, charging her to stay where she was until he came to fetch her, she remained serenely blinking in the sun, her only care to wonder if, when he came again, it would be to convey her straight to Buckingham Palace ; for it would be nice if she could wash her face and hands first.

The dog jumped into the hansom with a carriage-folk deportment, and the driver congratulated himself, and refrained from any injunctions about the seat ; for any one going to such an expensive address at this hour of the morning would be sure to give a good tip. The tip was all he had hoped, and before he drove off he gave an approving glance to the newly painted house-front, the window-boxes, and the mahogany door which the young man had slammed behind him so briskly.

' Oh hang ! I shouldn't have slammed it. Wake every one in the house,' he was saying as he ran upstairs. He knocked lightly on a bedroom door. There was no answer and he entered, followed by the dog, who walked with assurance to a corner, cast himself down, sighed piously, and fell asleep. Drawing back the curtains, he stood for a moment admiring the arching pattern of the tree-tops in the Square gardens. Then he turned towards the bed. A young woman lay there. She was awake, and looked at him with clear eyes. It was evident from the likeness between them that they were brother and sister.

'Darling, how obliging of you to be awake! I never like to disturb any one if I can help it.'

'Is anything the matter?'

'Nothing whatever.'

He seated himself on the foot of the bed, looked at the pillows, sighed with great artistry and then yawned unfeignedly. The young woman took his hand, regarding him affectionately and intently.

'When is your next waiting?' he inquired.

'I go to her on Tuesday.'

'Tuesday. . . . I think she is very lucky to have you.'

'Did you really come in at this hour to ask me about my waiting?'

Another yawn prevented the answer.

'Constantine, why do you spend the night dancing with little wretches?'

'Because they dance so much better than little worthies. You know, Emily, you are a moral snob. If I had spent the night dancing at Lambeth Palace—doesn't the Archbishop give balls? Stingy fellow, then, keeping his gaiters to himself—if I had spent the night dancing at Lambeth Palace you would be delighted with me. Because I spend it at Covent Garden you pull a long face. But you needn't My behaviour is as blameless in the one place as it would be at the other. In fact, now I come to consider it, it is more blameless. I don't tell half so many lies, and I pay for my supper.'

'Goose, go to bed! Besides, it's bad for the Lotus Bloom to keep him up till all hours.'

'Shan't! Besides, he likes it. He sits observing the animal creation in the form of donkeys. So you go into waiting on Tuesday, do you? Where? Here, or at Windsor?'

'We go to Windsor on Friday.'

He nodded his head thoughtfully.

'It strikes me, Emily, that we don't think enough of the old lady.'

'I am very fond of her.'

'Fond, yes. So am I fond of Nanny or old Graves. Bless their crusty old hearts, I can't imagine the British Constitution without them. But, Emily, she's more than that. She is England's Queen, she is something very fine indeed. Perhaps we shall never know how fine. We are too much accustomed to her, we see her too close. England's Queen isn't meant to be looked at close. But one day, later on, some time in the twentieth century, people will look back. And there she'll be, sitting up against the horizon like St. Paul's, blue and majestic and dumpy; but superbly dumpy, sitting there bolt upright with her crown on, dwarfing and mothering everything.   And we, we who live in her reign, we shall all be underneath, we shall be under the dome.'

He spoke with enthusiasm, wriggling his long legs, his eyes suddenly alight.   The glow faded off his face as swiftly as it had shone there ; he sighed, rumpled his hair, and tapped with his foot on the floor like a spirited horse that chafes at long standing still.   Emily sat up and kissed her brother.

' Dearest Constantine, you do have the most beautiful ideas.   I could never have thought of all that.'

' Neither could I.   I owe all that to Miss Bond.'

' Miss Bond ? '

' Miss Bond.   Miss Bond, who is now waiting for us to fetch her from Covent Garden Market. Miss Bond, for whom you are going to procure an audience with Her Majesty.   Miss Bond, who came up to London to see the Queen, travelling in a grove of parsley and marjoram, and who must be wanting her breakfast pretty badly (she likes her tea strong).   So now, dear Emily, ask no more questions, but put on your bonnet, and hazard your reputation by driving with me in a cab to Covent Garden—it's a very pretty countrified place at this hour—and we will bring her back with us.'

'My dear, what are you talking about? My head goes round and round.'

'I will explain everything in the cab. Now I will only say this: that I promise you I am not asking you to do anything you would afterwards wish undone.'

'No, of course not. But I don't understand why it is that——'

'When you see her you will understand.'

'Is she so very beautiful?'

'I don't know. I don't think she's beautiful. She is like——she is like a feather, any small feather the wind blows along the ground. You pick it up, you look at it casually. And then it is as though you had never looked at anything before, it is so perfect, so finished, so intent on being a feather, so—so——' he waved his hand impatiently. 'Oh, fairies, Ruskin, anything you like. You will come, won't you?'

'Come? Of course I'll come. And now will you please make yourself more respectable? I don't want people to say: "There's that unfortunate Emily Melhuish actually eloping in a hired cab with a waiter."'

He was gone, scampering down the passage;

but in a moment the door opened again, and he said : 'I haven't an idea what it is she wants to say to her. But don't let us ask. We won't finger the feather, will we ? '

Even had they been less aristocratically unworldly, Constantine and Emily Melhuish would have been no match for Sukey. At Halfacres and during the journey it might seem the most rational thing in the world for a loyal young woman in difficulties to apply to a monarch who was a woman too, but at the first question the conviction had darted upon her that this was a project demanding the nicest handling, a broth to be stirred by one cook alone. So far, things had fallen out admirably ; it was not every poor servant girl, she thought with a glow of elected pride, who would so promptly find a gentleman so willing and affable with a sister who was a lady-in-waiting ; it would be a pity to hazard these advantages by too great a flow of confidence. People, even the most promising people, had, she knew, a way of listening to one's plans only to put forward other plans of their own, plans which would naturally seem to them a great deal better. If Lady Emily were to put forward a plan, politeness and gratitude would oblige her to declare it an improvement ; and once you have given way to the improver you never know where it will lead you : it might even end in a conclusion that the best plan would be for her to give up all thought of marrying Eric. Yes, she must walk circumspectly, be on her guard, keep her own counsel still; even to the Queen, perhaps, it might be as well not to enter too lavishly into all her reasons for wanting that Bible.

Perhaps she had, unavowed to herself, a further reason for secrecy. Since the moment when, with Prudence's story burning in her ears, she had looked at The True Secret and beheld a vision, she had believed implicitly that Eric could be hers by barter. It would have been impiety to doubt it, to question the working of a stratagem put into her heart, she verily believed, by some good angel, wrestled with and overcome into blessing by the compulsion of her wretchedness—or if the stratagem was a little too artful to be fathered on an angel, then it was Love that had inspired it, Love whose strong wings will stoop to any cunning, any unscrupulous sorcery. Whether of Love or of an angel, the stratagem was certainly inspired ; she was not by herself able to conceive such a scheme, lofty as a cloud, exact as a mouse-trap. For what could be more ingeniously infallible ? It all fitted together like the pieces in a puzzle. Mrs Seaborn bowed beneath a royal slight; a royal hand bestowing

Bibles; Sukey Bond, a lover despised by the mother of her love, that proud creature whose pride now only whetted her disgrace. But Sukey Bond, bearing a Bible from the Queen, still with a shine about her, like Moses from the mountain, would be no longer despicable; she would then be in a position to say: 'Here is rehabilitation, here is your honour fresh from the hand of a Queen, here is beauty for ashes. Now give me my due. Give me Eric, a fair exchange.'

All that was needed was the Bible; and now she was near to getting it, so near that she dared not for one moment allow any doubt, any criticism, to deflect her from her purpose. She must not unfold her plan. Even approval of it, should others approve, might distract her, might throw her off her balance. And disapproval—if it were only spoken disapproval, she thought she could weather that, and go on with a stiffened determination, a head held higher; but people could act their disapproval, could clash those iron gates in her face, bid those fixed bayonets level their steel glance at her, send a policeman to take her to prison, a warder to carry Eric to the madhouse. Not only could they: she knew only too well that there was a great likelihood that they would; for people have strong views on such matters as hers: they disapprove when a servant-girl marries a gentleman, and they might further—for all she knew—disapprove when an idiot marries a servant-girl.

These were open terrors. She had not come so far without looking them in the face. They were, when all was said and done, only the disbelief of others, the common obstacle, the common enmity; and common discretion should be able to armour her against them. But suppose that she herself should begin to disbelieve? It was not enough to ward off the criticisms of others. She must keep her own at bay, lest in some unguarded moment she should find herself examining her own heart with the unbelief of a stranger. Then all would be lost: the vision a cheat, the stratagem neither of Love nor the angel, but the day-dream of a silly girl.

The more she resolved upon the propriety of not answering too many questions, the more clearly did she perceive how unlikely it was that no questions would be asked; and her knees weakened under her when, bidden to the morning-room, she found herself alone with Lady Emily, and heard a voice, alarming in its kindness, say: 'Now, Sukey, you must tell me all about yourself.' But Lady Emily's questions, though peculiar, were such as could be answered in perfect tranquillity of mind, nor did she seem to be one of those people with plans ; for though when she heard about the orphanage she said : 'Oh dear !' and on learning that the Reverend Mulberry Glossop wore a starched surplice and recited the Creed without turning to the East, 'Oh dear !' again, she made no suggestions as to how all this could be remedied. 'Poor lamb !' she exclaimed with feeling : an endearment that, from a lady's lips, surprised Sukey, until Lady Emily enlarging it into 'Poor shepherdless lamb !' she understood it to be a religious endearment.

In the housekeeper's room curiosity was more practical, and questions brisker, and her tormentors terribly ready to supplement her answers with glosses of their own. They intended her no ill, her concerns meant little to them ; but they had a lively, well-fed, traditional interest in the affairs of their employers, and Sukey was to them another manifestation of the dramatic doings of Lord Constantine and Lady Emily. Sukey lost her head, and was beginning to lose her temper, when she was snatched out of their clutches by a timely fit of hysterics. Once more she found herself alone with Lady Emily, but this interview took place in the butler's pantry where she had been carried for air.

'It's the suspense,' Lady Emily declared, kneeling on the stone flags as if a dress fashion-

ably tight about the knees were nothing to her,
and dabbing Sukey's face with a lace handkerchief sopped in vinegar from the salad cruet.
' Of course it is the suspense. But you shall see
her. She is so kind, I know she will receive you.
And meanwhile you had better go to bed. I
always go to bed if I am in the slightest anxiety.'

After that there was a great deal of bed, and no
more questions. There were also expeditions to
the Zoological Gardens, Madame Tussaud's, the
Tower of London, and a strangely-behaved
church where Lady Emily knelt as recklessly as
in the butler's pantry. All her life long Sukey
remembered Lord Constantine walking among
the bears, twirling a wooden spoon that dripped
with treacle. There was also an expedition—
but this was unaccompanied—to the pillar-box
at the corner, and two mornings later an envelope
with the Dannie postmark. There was no
flourish beneath Prudence's signature now, and
her letter was short.

> *Dear Suke,*
>
> *She went off about ten days ago and took him with
> her. She's left no address, the Bank is forwarding
> the letters. But Mr Morley at the station says she
> took tickets to somewhere called Morton St Ellery.
> It's in Hertfordshire, he says. That's all.*
>
> *Prudence.*

' Letter from home ? ' suggested the cook.

' From a friend.'

There were no more suggestions. ' If you fetch my young lady down again, that won't be the last of it,' remarked Mrs Cole, who governed her nurseling's household with the swagger of a viceroy. ' And the girl is a nice quiet old-fashioned girl, not like these modern young flimsy-gigs, too fanciful to tie their own cap-ribbons. I like her. And so does Master Muff.' Below-stairs the blue dog was called Muff, respect-fully. The gentry, Mrs Cole ruled, could call the dear animal what they pleased, being educated ac-cording ; but she would not have any one under her cockering themselves up with foreign words they had no right to.

It was Mrs Cole, wearing discretion and relia-bility like a rich glaze, who went with her in the carriage to the Palace. She glanced at Sukey's hands. They were quivering slightly. ' Take off your gloves for a minute or two,' she said. Sukey stared out of the window, searching the house-fronts for a clock ; she could recall every wavering of the two lines that Lady Emily had drawn under the words : *Be Punctual*. Mrs Cole extricated her gold watch and displayed it silently ; then, still without a word, she proffered a green bottle of smelling-salts. Words would have profaned her sense of competence. Beneath the rich glaze was a romantic fervour of pride, of capability, of excitement, a voluptuous glorying in being reliable and composed. If, instead of Sukey Bond, her mistress had commissioned her to escort a chimpanzee to Buckingham Palace, she would have carried out her orders in the same exaltation of humility, and if smelling-salts and the force of example could have done it, would have delivered over the animal in a very creditable frame of mind. But Sukey rejected the green bottle. 'Thank you, but I don't need them.'

This was a good girl, a girl with a head on her shoulders. She had said so all along. A good girl was going to see a good Queen—and that was just as it should be. The occasion was glorious, was unique, but was nothing to become flustered over ; and Mrs Cole remembered with a womanly smile the behaviour of her young master a few minutes since. She had not seen him put on quite that assumption of confidence and easy geniality since he was a little boy, and setting out for his first term at Eton. But no man, not even her young gentleman, could feel as comfortably about the Good Queen as any woman could, thought Mrs Cole, recalling that interview after which Constantine had lit a cigar and said to the blue dog : ' I should be able to take this more easily if I had money on it.'

In the moment between getting out of the carriage and entering the Palace, Sukey received a violent disjointed impression of what a fine day it was. The warmth of the air seemed in an instant to have clothed her with a new body ; she saw tree-tops above a wall, stirring under their May-time plumage with a wanton grace and laziness, and it was as if she had never seen such beings before ; she glanced up, and instead of looking at the blue sky, she thought she was looking into it. It was so real, this May morning, that it was almost unreal ; and as she crossed the threshold into the dusky and unsummered atmosphere of the Palace it remained in her dazzled eyes and swimming senses like something that she could never by any chance see again. Instead, she would always see these complicated vistas, these walls, so ornamented and yet so bleak, these vast and rather dingy perspectives, this dwelling that seemed as if it had never been meant for any one to dwell in, these strangers moving around her, unreal and sumptuous shadows. This was more dreamlike than any dream ; in all her anticipations she had not foreseen anything like this. For sometimes she had looked forward with certainty to the moment when her being would exclaim : Now I am in the Palace of the Queen of England ! and at others she had foreseen only a bondage of timidity and confusion. Now it seemed that she had ceased to exist as a creature sensible of human emotions, free only to move like a shadow among shadows ; as though not Sukey Bond but a tuft of thistle-down had floated in at the door which had closed behind her. Yet to the shadowy people she was real after a fashion, for they spoke her name, and admitted her purpose, one passing her on to another, bidding her pause here, or conducting her along passages and up a flight of stairs. It is these thick carpets, she thought, which make everything so queer. The passages were end-less. It was hours ago that she had left Nannie, sitting outside in the carriage, in the remote sun-light. Once she glanced from a window, ready to see Mrs Disbrowe standing among the dwindled houses ; and not seeing her, saw nothing. Once Lady Emily appeared beside her, looked at her solicitously, spoke to her, took her hand. Sukey answered the words, but had no notion what they were.

' You are to wait for Her Majesty in here.'

She heard that. One of the shadows had spoken, a nobleman or something ; and closing the door with a soft click he left her standing alone.

The room was lofty, rather cold, and smelt of furniture polish. It was full of a rich silence, the special silence of a palace—far away from the world, far above it—a silence without echoes, not like the silence of a church. What she could see of the room—for she remained standing exactly as the nobleman had left her—was this: a crimson carpet with garlands upon it of a paler crimson, part of a glistening white fur rug, the lower panels of a mahogany door, a velvet drapery, the carved and gilded base of a console table with a mirror behind it, and in the mirror the reflection of her own black boots planted upon the crimson carpet of a palace.

The boots did not fidget. By their immobility they were beginning to appear quite in place, as properly and reasonably there as the elegant swathes of the drapery or the gold claws of the console table. Above the claws rose up a strange female being: a slender arching body, two breasts, a face, two eyes looking out from the shadow. Wild, proud, mournful, and steadfast, the sphinx looked out from under the table with the look she had brought from Egypt. She was naked and half a beast; but Sukey, out of the tail of her eye, saw only something inscrutably sisterly, and took comfort from the presence of this woman who also had thoughts of her own.

' You are a woman.   Be secret,' the look said.
' Armour your breasts with secrecy.   Hold fast
with your claws.'

Sukey turned a little and smiled at the sphinx.
Above the reflected boots the hem of the new
skirt settled again into repose.   That morning
when Nannie had said : ' Here are the clothes
that Lady Emily wishes you to wear to-day,' she
had recalled the waxwork at Madame Tussaud's,
where a princess stooped her trailing splendours
to kiss the Queen's hand.   Perhaps, perhaps,
one might not visit the Queen except in robes
like these ; perhaps she too, for once in her life,
would wear satin, and white feathers, and a long
veil.   And when the parcel had disclosed a skirt
and a bodice only differing in newness and long-
wearingness from such as she ordinarily wore
she had known for a moment a more childish
disappointment than her childhood had ever
been allowed to know.   What foolishness, what
forgetfulness !   Such trimmings were for the
glorious, the guarded, the unbeseeching, who
kissed the Queen's hand, and went away to the
ball.   She was here upon a workaday errand, she
had more to do than to kiss hands.

The clock struck.   It was already the hour
that the Queen had appointed, and suddenly
Sukey knew herself destitute of time.   She might

come at any moment now. There was no more leisure to think, to plan, to call her wits about her. All those months of looking forward, so safe, so ample, had slid away and become the past. Why had she not thought more, planned better, rehearsed a speech, invented persuasions? Why had she fancied so boldly, so audaciously hoped? To bend a Queen into her stratagem, to use the Queen of England for her own purposes. Even now, she was wasting time in thinking time wasted; for surely a Queen would not be punctual? She saw the door-knob turn, the door slowly open. Two figures came sweeping into the room, the door closed again, and now her hour was come.

There were two ladies. One was tall and one was short, one had a rather haughty look and one was red-faced and homely. Both were dressed in black, and the white hands of both were glittering with jewels. But there could be no doubt as to which of them was the Queen.

A profound awe descended upon Sukey and cast out the meanness of fear. She was not flurried now; she forgot to fancy herself unprepared, she forgot her preparations. As if she had been grafted into some unknown ceremony, she discovered herself knowing exactly what to do : this was to fall upon her knees, and presently, slowly, to raise her head and look the Queen in the face. Very searchingly and without a word the Queen looked back at her. A feeling like tears overwhelmed Sukey as she received that serious and searching look. She forgot all her imagination of what a Queen would be like, she forgot the sleek solemnity of The True Secret and the young Queen on the sixpenny pieces—slender and severe ; she forgot her first impression of redness and homeliness. In the face before her she saw what obliterated all these : the indelible aspect of sorrow. Age and sorrow had trapped the face of a child : the eyes that regarded her with a child's solemn attention and curiosity flowered out of a flesh that was as if trampled and bruised with cares and weeping and watchfulness, and two deeply trenched furrows guarded the small childish half-open mouth.

The Queen seated herself, and motioned with her hand towards the window. The lady opened it, and the noise of London came in as if it were speaking to the Queen.

' Please get up,' she said, ' and come nearer to me. I am tired, and I cannot speak loud.'

Her voice was remarkably low and clear, the voice of the young Queen on the sixpenny pieces.

Sukey approached and stood waiting to hear it again.

'I know who you are,' the Queen continued. 'You are Sukey Bond. Now tell me what it is that you have come to ask me.'

'If you please, Your Majesty, I want something that only you can give. That is why I am so bold. . . .'

Her voice wavered with her wavering courage. Hearing herself speaking to the Queen she began to understand the extent of her daring. Nor was speaking to the Queen all. Indeed, it was the least part of it, since what she had come to say involved leaving so much unspoken.

'Go on,' said the Queen. 'Don't be afraid. I think you are a good young woman, and if that is so, you have nothing to fear.'

'Your Majesty, I have come about a lady, the wife of the Rector of Southend. She is called Mrs Seaborn. Your Majesty, Mrs Seaborn believes she has offended you, and nothing can comfort her. She thinks that you are angry with her, Your Majesty.'

'Seaborn?' said the Queen; and turning to the lady-in-waiting she repeated the name in a questioning tone. The lady replied, but her voice was mumbling and Sukey could not hear what she said.

The Queen turned again to Sukey. Her look was serious and puzzled, the look of a good child puzzling over a sum.

'I cannot make this out. Why should Mrs Seaborn think she has offended me?'

'I do not know, Your Majesty. She is a lady, I cannot speak for her reasons. I only know this—that she can think of nothing else, only that you are angry with her. She won't see any one, she hides herself away for shame, and every day she grows more low-spirited. No one can comfort her, no one but you, Your Majesty. That is why I have come.'

The Queen looked grave, and said: 'I am afraid you have hoped too much. I do not see what I can do.'

'Your Majesty, I have seen a picture of you giving away a Bible to a poor savage. When I heard about Mrs Seaborn I thought of that picture, I said to myself: I will go and ask the Queen. If I were to carry her a Bible from the Queen's own hand, she would look up.'

The lady-in-waiting had begun to simmer discreetly; it was clear that she wanted to say something. When the Queen questioned her she began to whisper and shake her head. Sukey caught one word: 'Mad.'

Mad. That was what people might say about

Eric. The word was like the thrust of a knife; she felt her courage, her hopes, her wits, bleeding out of the wound in her brain. Had she said too much, had she given her secret away? She tried to remember what she had said, but the noise of London came in, bellowing like the sea, and washed away all articulate recollection. She discovered that she was glaring at the lady-in-waiting, that her hands twitched to claw and strangle, that her body rocked stiffly like the body of a cat about to spring; but they were talking, and did not heed her. Before their unconsciousness her defiance cowered down and was extinct. She did not try to listen now, she looked about her, listlessly measuring her loneliness. Then she caught sight of the sphinx.

'But has this Mrs Seaborn no one to send but you?'

'She did not send me, Your Majesty; she would not dare to do such a thing. No one sent me, I came of myself.'

'You did not consult with anybody before you set out? Not with her relations, not with her husband?'

'Your Majesty, he is dead. Mrs Seaborn is a widow.'

The Queen sighed. But as though she were

locking away her own thoughts, she questioned Sukey with even keener glances.

'Her children, then; are you sure they did not put this idea into your head?'

For a moment Sukey hesitated. She feared to lie, she would always rather prevaricate; and her conscience told her that if it had not been for her love for Eric she would not now be standing before the Queen of England.

'Lie!' commanded the sphinx.

'No, Your Majesty.'

But her voice betrayed the uneasiness of her thought, and as though she suspected something the Queen asked her sharply:

'Has she children, this Mrs Seaborn?'

'Your Majesty, she has one son.'

'And this son; what of him?'

The sphinx could prompt her no longer. Bewildered, deadly afraid, scarcely knowing what she said, Sukey replied:

'Please, Your Majesty. . . . I am afraid he is not a comfort to her, just now.'

The Queen sighed once more, sighed profoundly. And this time she did not seem able to lock her own thoughts away. She sat for a long while in silence, looking down at her ringed white hands lying on her black lap, and all the childishness ebbed from her face, stealing off, a scared child, from the presence of this care-worn old woman. At last she looked up, as though she was come back from far away to see with surprise Sukey Bond standing before her. She drew herself up, and said to the lady-in-waiting :

'Bring me a Bible.'

A Bible, a Bible bound in black leather, a Bible with the Queen's handwriting blackening upon the black end-paper : *For a loyal subject, Victoria R.* She had got it at last, as surely as though she were a heathen it was hers. Mrs Cole had admired it, and Lord Constantine had admired it, and Master Muff had snuffed at it with what might have been admiration, and now it lay on her lap, a dream embodied, and something that she must be careful not to cry over. For her triumph had turned on her and was remorse. She had deceived the Queen, behaving in a most underhand and disloyal fashion to a Sovereign who was so gracious, to an old lady who was so sorrowful. She dared not open the Bible, for fear that some text about liars and cozeners should pop out on her, and yet she would have liked to read, for reading might have plugged her uneasy conscience and dulled her ears to the words which rang there with such uncomfortable reality. 'I hope you will always do your duty,' the Queen had said, staring up into Sukey's face ; and then, grunting softly at the effort of lifting herself from her seat, she had left the room and taken her powers and her cares with her.

Sukey could bear the weight of that Bible no longer. She put it away, and washed her face severely. This was what love brought one to ; to deceitfulness and cunning and shamelessness. I wonder who I shall have to deceive next, she thought ; for though she had got the Bible she had not yet got Eric, and until she had him there would be no end to this weltering in artfulness, this massacre of principles. And immediately it was clear whom she would have to deceive next ; her hosts, these gentle gentlefolk, who had taken her in, and indulged her secretiveness, and smoothed her path to the Queen ; for it was certain that they would not let her go without considerable solicitude as to where she was going. Well, if they made difficulties, there was nothing for it but to run away. She could run away from Lowndes Square too.

As it was, she went away in a perfectly respectable and countenanced manner with Mrs Cole to see her safely into the train at St Pancras. Matters might not have gone so smoothly if Lady Emily had been at home, but she was still in waiting, and so Sukey had addressed herself to

Lord Constantine, whose experience in questioning people for their good was not such as to
make his questions very redoubtable. Sukey
was quick to discover this, and allowed herself
the unusual luxury of answering truthfully.

'But isn't Morton St Ellery in Hertfordshire?'
he said. 'I thought it was Essex that you came
from. Or perhaps you are just passing through
London.'

'I came from Essex, Lord Constantine. But
that was only my place.'

'Oh. Oh, I see.'

'Where I was in service, Lord Constantine.'

'Exactly. And now you are going to your
home?'

'To my mother-in-law.'

She saw him instantly avert his eyes from her
left hand.

'To be,' she added.

It would have been tempting Providence to
incline her ear to the kind wishes, congratula-
tions, and inquiries she saw impending; it would
also have been tempting Lord Constantine to ask
something inconvenient; so she stemmed him
civilly. It was one of the pleasant things about
real gentry, such as these, that they were so
easily stemmed: the smallest little hint was
enough for them. This was the moment for an

audacity that she had been polishing ever since she got up that morning.

'If it would not be taking too great a liberty, do you think that Lady Emily would accept of this? Maybe it would sometimes put her in mind of one she was so kind to.'

The speech came out almost as smooth and round as the little pink box that the tramp had given her.

'*Friendship endears*,' he read, holding it poised on the palm of his hand, and looking at it as though it were a peacock butterfly. 'I'm sure my sister will like this very much indeed. Pink is her favourite colour.'

Sukey exclaimed in an irresistible burst of affection:

'I wish that I had something I could give you!'

'When you are married, and keep a hive of bees, you can send me some honey.'

When you are married. When you are married and keep a hive of bees. The heavenly words danced in her brain, and the rattle of the four-wheeler, and Mrs Cole's parting admonitions, and the rumble of the train were so many comfortable basses over which this theme might point its toes. When you are married. He had actually said married, he had spoken aloud the word that was her secret thought, he had accepted her marriage and her mother-in-law as being quite in the natural course of things. When you are married and keep a hive of bees—it was like some gayer kind of *whom God hath joined together*, the words as good as wedded her. She smiled so joyously, and leaned out of the window so constantly, to see if this station was Morton St Ellery or if that cottage had a bee-skep in its garden, that the old lady in the corner seat in whom Mrs Cole had placed so much reliance began to look annoyed and to draw in her feet rebukingly. But Sukey did not heed her; she noticed nothing of her save that she was old and did not look out of the window. Indeed she was happy enough to upset any old lady who paid income-tax and disliked railway travelling. She had forgotten her remorse of overnight, she had got her Bible; she had never in all her life felt so frisky, unless it were on that evening when Eric asked her to marry him and they ran races over the marsh. The train was a slow train, and stopped at all the stations, but to Sukey it seemed to go with the speed of the wind. She was set out on the third, the last, the gloriously crowning last stage of her journey towards Eric. She had walked to Southend, she had ridden to London in a waggon; now she was going by train, a fiery monster of enormous power and explosiveness was hastening her onward to her

love, and the children who ran out to watch its
passing seemed to waft her on her course with
their fluttering handkerchiefs. She pulled out
her own to return their greeting.

'Ah! I thought you would be getting a grit
in your eye,' muttered the old lady. But the
tiresome girl had nothing in her eye, and went on
waving. Really these young chits should not be
allowed to travel alone. It was a mercy when
she got out at Morton St Ellery.

Mr Warburton, whose mother had by the
simple act of dying given being to the Warburton
Memorial Female Orphanage, possessed, unknown to Sukey, an estate at Morton St Ellery ;
and that was why, standing on the platform,
Sukey could see no trace of human habitation
beyond two coal-offices, a house agent's notice-
board, and a small booth labelled *Hairdresser and
Tobacconist*. All else was green fields. For Mr
Warburton would have no smoke poisoning
his trees, no sparks setting alight to his park-
land, no whistles disturbing his guests and causing
his pedigree ewes to bring forth their young un-
timely. The damned branch line could know its
place ; it would do the villagers no harm to walk,
and as for the parson, he would give the fellow
a lift occasionally—for in these disestablishing
days one must stand by the cloth.

' Matter of two miles by road,' the porter said. ' But if you don't mind a stile or two, you can go the field way, and shorten it. I'll see to your box meanwhile.'

To be carrying a Bible and walking through fields was like going to church in The Fairchild Family. But no member of that family had ever walked with such unchastened sensations of happiness, nor carried, Sukey reflected with a toss of pride, a Bible with the Queen's name in it. It was full afternoon; the shadows delved a larger shade under the elms, the warmed may-blossom gave out its scent of almonds, the cows moved more heavily among the buttercups, feeling the weight of their milk. Half-grown lambs played as they had played all day, leaping and buffeting each other with intuitive wantonness, then abruptly galloping off to tug at their mothers. Presently the warmth of the air would become a visible powder of gold, and the blackbirds and thrushes would begin singing. There was no hurry in these broad fields, but time to smell the may-blossom, and talk to the cows, and rest oneself, and dawdle over the choice of a place to rest in. Where were the buttercups thickest? Would it be pleasanter to sit in the shade or in the sun?

She tossed up the Holy Bible and caught it

again, and tossed it higher and caught it that time too. It was joy to be alive, to feel the sun, to be near her lover. This air here, so gentle and so gay, it was as though it breathed him. And soon she would be nearer. In an hour's time maybe, she would have delivered over the Bible and won him in exchange. But there was no hurry in these broad fields, her delight was ample enough to allow for delay. Perhaps if she waited a little he might come into the field and find her. That would be sweetest.

A small thicket of hawthorns straggled out from the hedge, and a lamb lay under it, poured out in sleep. She sat down beside it, and stretched herself and yawned from happiness and silliness. If Eric were to come to her now he would like the lamb. She tried to fancy his coming : how he would first appear, strolling idly, even a little sadly, bare-headed, tilting his face this way and that to the sun ; and then he should see her—though that must be of his own accord, for she would be sitting as still as a mouse, all her being summed up in attention, tremblingly compact like a drop of dew hanging on a spray ; and then, when he had seen her, she would hold out her arms, and he would run to her, run with such haste that for once in his life he would be almost clumsy. And then, and then—her imagination flickered, and she went back to the beginning again. Her excitement would not allow her to think steadfastly, even of him. She began to make a daisy chain, and when she had plaited a few inches of it she tired, and flicked it lightly over the lamb's back, and wondered what to do next. The Bible lay beside her, she thought she would look at the Queen's name once more. It was tied up into a neat parcel, but she unknotted the string and unfolded the wrappings. Here in the field the Bible appeared intensely black, and its smell of Sunday sobriety was astonishingly pungent. It must have been the smell which alarmed the lamb, who woke with a start, looked wildly round and fled bleating, with the daisy chain dangling from its rump. When her eye had learned every loop in the Queen's name, Sukey ran her finger across the pages, enjoying their crisp rustle, and admiring their changing colour, red or gold as they slipped under her finger. Odd words caught her eye and were gone : *Gershom*, *Kohath*, *and Mehari*, *transgressions*, *cucumber*, *verity and judgment*. She stayed her hand at random and looked into the page. *The church's graces*, she read. *Her faith and desire.*

How fair and how pleasant art thou, O love, for delights !

This thy stature is like to a palm tree, and thy breasts to clusters of grapes.

I said, I will go up to the palm tree, I will take hold of the boughs thereof : now also thy breasts shall be as clusters of the vine, and the smell of thy nose like apples ;

And the roof of thy mouth like the best wine for my beloved, that goeth down sweetly, causing the lips of those that are asleep to speak.

I am my beloved's, and his desire is toward me.

Come, my beloved, let us go forth into the field ; let us lodge in the villages.

Let us get up early to the vineyards ; let us see if the vine flourish, whether the tender grape appear, and the pomegranates bud forth : there will I give thee my loves.

The mandrakes give a smell, and at our gates are all manner of pleasant fruits, new and old, which I have laid up for thee, O my beloved.

She could read no further, reading of love. Her senses were confused, her limbs were heavy with an unknown and ravishing darkness, a tide of languor that flowed through her body, loosening her joints, dissolving her flesh, melting and kindling through her, drowsily smouldering along her side. The almond smell of the may-blossom seemed to bow down and enclose her, the smell of mandrakes, sweetly-sickly as the

275

smell of a love philtre; with every breath she drew it into her and made its voluptuous tranquillity her own, with every breath she relinquished her consciousness in exchange for this dusk of the spirit. She seemed to float upon her breathing as a ship floats upon the waves. Infinitely removed she saw the Bible, and all her cares, and all her scheming, and all her resolution and her artfulness. This abandonment, this fathomless peace, was what lay beneath it all, this was what lay at the core of love. She thought to laugh, and uttered instead a sound between a grunt and a sigh; and then, settling herself more deeply into the ground, she gave herself up and fell asleep.

'Sukey, Sukey! Wake up.'

It was like passing from sleep into a dream to open her eyes and find him bending over her. She put up her arms to draw him down to her.

'O Sukey, my darling! Get up, you must come quickly, you must hide.'

His voice was anxious, his kiss light and undemanding; only his eyes caressed her.

'Darling, what is it, what is the matter?'

'Be quick! Be quick! Here, behind these bushes. We can hide here.'

He drew her into a nook in the hedge, where the hawthorns screened them from the path, and put his arm round her. She was about to question him when he laid his finger on her lips.

'Hush, hush! Don't move, don't say a word. She mustn't know you are here.'

Bewildered and at a loss, she turned her attention to the only thing that mattered to her : to him. He was more comely even than her remembrance of him, but he was changed. He was taller and thinner than of old, he had lost his freckles, there were shadows under his eyes and a faint puzzled wrinkle had come into his forehead. He looked, she thought, as though he needed petting, and she longed to take him in her arms. But his manner forbade it. He peered through the bushes, turning his head with small rapid movements, like a bird. Suddenly she felt his arm tremble, and close more tightly about her, and heard him catch his breath.

Mrs Seaborn had entered the field. Her widow's weeds trailed over the buttercups, she wore black gloves and held up a sunshade. She walked slowly and strayingly, not keeping to the path. At first Sukey thought she must be looking for Eric, for at every few steps she stopped dead, turned her head a little over her left shoulder, and stared. Thus wandering and stopping and wandering on again, she approached them until she was near enough for her features to be seen.   Sukey beheld them and was plunged into terror.

For Mrs Seaborn was not looking for Eric. She was not looking for any one. While she walked her face was vacant and lowering ; when she stopped, turning her head always to the same degree over her shoulder, it was suddenly, blindly contorted into a grimace of furious pride and hatred.   Slowly the mask would blur, would slacken, would swim into vacancy again ; and she would walk on, her widow's veil waving back into place, her parasol bobbing slightly with the inequalities of the ground.

Mrs Seaborn was a madwoman.

Sukey remembered Prudence's story. ' And then the Princess, she gave Mrs Seaborn that look.' That look which had so festered into Mrs Seaborn's pride that now it possessed her like a demon, and glared out from her sick brain where it sat gnawing her.   Yes, she must act it out, over and over again, that look.

Now she was close to them, so close that Sukey could see that her cheeks were raddled with a horrible pink, and her spoiled lips painted. It was then that Sukey remembered the Bible, lying right in Mrs Seaborn's path.   She had seen it. She stopped, she put down her sunshade with elegant deliberation, she bent with a sweeping movement of extraordinary grace and picked it up. She read the title carefully, and then began turning over the pages with an expression of polite interest. She was reading it back- wards, in a moment she would come to the end-paper and the inscription. She let it fall as a baby lets fall its rattle, put up her sun- shade once more and moved on; and at the third step she stood still, turned her head over her shoulder and glared unseeingly at the hawthorn-brake.

So she passed out of sight, her veil waving behind her, wandering and stopping and wander- ing on again. And at length Eric sighed, and kissed Sukey and whispered: 'Stay here while I see if she's gone.'

She would have stayed him from danger, but it was too late. She sank down among the bushes, bruised and sickened with terror. And Eric had been under the shadow of this while she had dawdled at Halfacres, and lived softly in Lowndes Square. He came running back, and knelt down beside her.

'She's gone,' he said. 'Now she will go home.' Suddenly he laid his head in her bosom and clung to her.

'O Sukey, I was so afraid. I thought she would kill you.'

' Eric, you can't stay here. I am going to take you away.'

She felt him shake his head against her breast.

' Come, my darling, my poor love. She shall never frighten you again.'

' But where shall we go ? '

She rose to her feet.

' We will go to the Queen.'

Hand in hand they walked from the field, and the Queen's Bible lay open on the grass where Mrs Seaborn had let it fall. The wind of evening ruffled the pages over, and presently an enterprising spider began to march across the fifth chapter of Deuteronomy. If it had been an ordinary book, he would most probably have gone down the tunnel at the back ; but as it was a Bible, and he an insect of character, he essayed the overland route.

Absorbed in each other's company, Eric and Sukey scarcely noticed that they had quitted the field path, and were come out into a lane. They said little to each other, and such speech as they exchanged was casual and inexplicit—a sort of nudging, a grace-note to companionship. An oak-tree gleaming in its new foliage, the flight of some rooks, a child at a cottage door who stood to watch them, careless of the struggles of the kitten which she held pressed to her pinafore—

to acknowledge them was enough, admitting them into their silence merely as an affirmation that they walked together. 'See those rooks?' 'I like a ginger kitten, don't you?' And then an agreement, and then silence again.

So they had walked together in the marsh, half a year ago. It seemed now to Sukey that since parting from Eric she had talked incessantly, that those five months had been spent in a feverish conversation with her own thoughts, such a conversation, frantic, urgent, and un-meaning, as one holds with a stranger in a dream. Now she could be quiet again, now her thoughts could wander uninterrogated while her body kept step with his.

But walking together in the marsh they had walked through a landscape of autumn, berried hedges whence the starlings flew up like a handful of dust thrown into the air to fall and settle again, and over ploughed fields and fields where the stubble glittered metallically. Silently Eric had handed her blackberries while the sea-gulls cried overhead. They had walked under waning skies, making the most of the weakening sun, pulling the dusk round them, as they sat together, like a cloak. Now they were walking through a world made into a bower, and for the seagulls and the one winter robin they had the rustle of young grown things and all the spring birds. And Eric was picking her a nosegay.

He had scrambled into the hedge, and she stood in the roadway, looking at the shape of a leaf against the sky, listening to the whisper and soft scrabble of the boughs he brushed against, thinking that it was he, he himself, who caused those sounds, tasting her happiness. She heard the pacing steps of a horse approaching them, and the margin of her mind knew that the rider was a gentleman. She moved to one side and at the same moment the horse stopped, and a voice said:

' Haven't I seen you before ? '

She raised her eyes to a recollection ; and there once more was Mr Warburton, regarding her exactly as he had regarded her over the prize-laden table on that hot afternoon at the orphanage when he had so surprisingly cast off the god and accosted her as a human being.

' Haven't I seen you before ? ' Those were then his very words, and spoken then as he spoke them now ; as though he were a trifle bewildered at this human contact, as though, for all his majesty, having unbent, he looked round for support and reassurance. Once more Sukey dropped a curtsey ; but this time there was no Miss Pocock present to vouch for her so she was obliged to speak for herself.

' If you please, sir, I am Sukey Bond.'

Hearing her voice, Eric jumped down from the hedge and placed himself in front of her.

' She is my Sukey who has come back to me. And no one shall frighten her for we mean to be married.'

Since the murder was out she would put a bold face on it. Besides, though Eric's words were gallant his voice was nervous and defiant. She stepped forward and put her arm through his, all the while steadfastly regarding Mr Warburton.

' Spoken like a man, Eric. I'm glad you know your own mind.'

Suddenly Sukey recalled how Mrs Seaborn was so notable among the lady patronesses because she was related to Mr Warburton. He was more than a gentleman on horseback now ; he was a relation. But there was little space for fear in this meeting where speech followed speech, discovery discovery, as pat as cards falling from the dealer's hand.

Mr Warburton took out his watch and read the time, raising his eyebrows with a sort of condescending surprise as if Time were a kitten to him, a kitten whose leaps and pranks he found entertaining.

He addressed Sukey once more.

' Where are you two off to ? '

' We are going to the Queen,' answered Eric.

' Come and see me instead.'

He turned the horse and rode slowly up the lane. The smell of his cigar hung on the air, strong and bland, an invisible portion of Mr Warburton. Presently he turned in at the drive gate, and the lodge-keeper came out and bowed to the three of them.

The house they entered was so exceedingly magnificent that Sukey might have been daunted had she not remembered that only the day before yesterday she had visited Buckingham Palace, a thought which enabled her to look round upon any splendours with composure. However, they stayed indoors no longer than to eat some hot-house grapes ; then at Mr Warburton's suggestion they went off to inspect the Home Farm and the piggeries. Before the pigsties even Buckingham Palace lost some of its power to reassure, for each pig had a white china dwelling to itself with a white paved forecourt, and couched upon quantities of the cleanest golden straw, as though a lady loved it. They were white pigs with short turned-up noses and expressions of such amiability that it seemed impossible that, even at feeding-time, a rude word should make itself heard among them. Only the sucklings were a delicate pink, clustered about their mother's belly like cherubs on a monument.

For some time none of them spoke. Eric had somehow possessed himself of a switch and was scratching a sow behind the ear. At length Sukey said softly : ' Do you remember the little pigs at New Easter ? ' The sound of her voice roused Mr Warburton to a sense of action ; he propelled her further along to a neighbouring sty, coughed and remarked :

' This is an odd set-out.'

Sukey thought that one of the oddest aspects of the set-out was Mr Warburton's philosophical reception of it ; but she had no objection to that, and waited to hear what more he had to say.

' I 've heard something about you already, Sukey, from Mrs Seaborn.'

' What did Mrs Seaborn tell you ? '

Mr Warburton hesitated. ' We won't go into all that,' he said. ' Mrs Seaborn is sometimes rather prejudiced. As a matter of fact, she is not quite—not quite herself, just at present. The loss of a husband, no doubt.'

' I saw Mrs Seaborn this afternoon.'

He stared at her, slowly pursing his lips.

' Whew ! '

' But not to speak to. I saw her walk through

a field. We saw her. Eric was with me, and we hid.'

' Exactly.'

Already it seemed a long way off, a long time ago, that figure watched through the blossoming hawthorn sprays ; and every moment Mrs Seaborn receded further from reality, a creature wandering in the uncreditable, unauthentic realm of the insane. It was not entirely duty which made Sukey say :

' It 's sad.'

Mr Warburton replied with disconcerting briskness : ' I daresay she 'll come round. Meanwhile,' he continued on a less confident note, ' there 's Eric. Now what are we to do about him ? '

Sukey knew quite well what she could do.

' When I met you two, I was on my way to look into it. For really when it comes to letters from my own parson drawing my attention to my own relations, it 's time to put a stop to it.'

' Yes, sir, I suppose it is.'

Mr Warburton drooped more heavily over the sty.

' It 's a serious responsibility, a young man like Eric on one's hands. I have a great many responsibilities.

' Something 's got to be done about it ! ' he exclaimed with decision.

Against her reason, against her caution, even against her sense of the proprieties, Sukey began to entertain the incredible idea that she was being entreated.   But still she hesitated to speak.

' A man,' said Mr Warburton firmly, ' is not the person to deal with Eric.   Eric needs handling.   How old are you ? '

' Nearly seventeen, sir.'

Mr Warburton's voice became even more firm.

' I should have said you were older than that.'

For a while he wooed her in silence, and Sukey listened to Eric talking to the sow.   She had no desire to hurry on this conversation, a conversation that she was finding increasingly enjoyable. For there could be no doubt, no doubt at all, as to the nature of Mr Warburton's insinuations— and she liked them.   Still, perhaps it would be civil to give him a helping hand.

' I think a country life would suit him best.'

' Certainly, certainly.   A country life would suit him infinitely best.   No other life would suit him at all.   Ah, I see you understand him.'

' A settled life.'

' Oh undoubtedly !   Nothing like a settled life. But the question I ask myself is : Who is to settle him ?

287

' Marriage.'

Mr Warburton breathed the word over the pigs.

' An excellent thing in woman.'

A pig's ear quivered. Such was the intensity of feeling in Mr Warburton's voice, Sukey could almost believe that she saw a blush run under those tight-fitting white bristles.

He moved a little nearer. He took hold of her left hand and considered it thoughtfully, touching her fingers, one, two, three.

' Are you prepared to marry Eric ? '

At these unexpected, these incredible words, she raised her head and looked, not at the questioner, but at her love. He felt her glance, turned his head, smiled. She held out her hands to him above the pigs. Overhead, an unheeded thunder, rang the loud jubilant voice of Mr Warburton's approval.

' Good girl ! Excellent girl ! Well, that 's settled, anyhow. Marry him as soon as you like, and leave all the rest to me. I will make the arrangements, cakes and clergy and what not. You can be done at the church here. Good fellow, Parson Highman, never known him anything but obliging. And I will give you away. You haven't got any relations, have you, to come bothering round ? Never does to have relations at weddings, can't think why people do have them. Unless it should be a brace or so of younger sisters for bridesmaids — don't mind them. If you'd like a bridesmaid or two you can have the gamekeeper's daughters. Well, that about settles the wedding, doesn't it? What would you like to do then?'

Being obliged by his silence to give a little attention to Mr Warburton, Sukey went through the ceremonies of thought: that is to say, she wrinkled her forehead and held her head on one side. But no thoughts emerged.

'What do you think would suit him best, sir?'

Mr Warburton was also going through the ceremonies of thought.

'Must be something in the country. How about a gentleman farmer?'

'That would never do.' Sukey spoke with decision. 'A farmer has to kill things.'

'Well, the Church then. How would it be if we were to clap him into a family living? He needn't kill anything there, unless it's a few greenfly on the roses.'

Sukey shook her head.

'I'm not so sure. Plenty of bishops not half so sensible as he. Besides, Seaborn was a parson, that sort of thing often runs in families. Eric, how would you like to go into the Church?'

' Go into the church ? ' Eric left the sow. ' Go into the church to marry Sukey ? But that isn't enough, you know. You must have a clergyman, and a ring, and call Banns. Sukey will tell you so.'

' You see,' she said softly.

' H'm ! He 's got a high opinion of Church ordinances, anyhow. Still, I daresay you 're right.'

Mr Warburton was beginning to look responsible once more, and to droop over the sty. Sukey felt that an effort was demanded of her. There must be something that she could suggest. There was.

' I believe that Eric would be good at keeping bees.'

Once again lightened of a responsibility, Mr Warburton rebounded into the sublime. But this time his approval was more majestic, more god-like.

' A happy thought, Sukey. A very happy thought. Bless me, what a sensible girl you are ! Bees be it.'

With a gesture that seemed to bless and encompass bees, pigs, the young moon, Eric and Sukey, all creation, he turned about and led the way back to Badger's Mount. It was dinner-time—a nobly consummated appetite told him so. Bees would do excellently well ; it was high time to come to a conclusion, and in many respects a beekeeper's life is to be preferred above the life of a farmer or a clergyman of the Church of England. For bees are in an especial manner dear to Jove, who in gratitude for that first sweetness taught them a policy and ordered living by which above all beasts and even man they exemplify majestic law : Virgil says so, speaking of the sky-born honey and the twice-yearly harvest, and their combats when the great hearts strain in the tiny breasts. Only they do not love ; that is left to their keepers—though in Mr Warburton's opinion there was little doubt but that the Corycian fellow was a bachelor. Yes, bees would do admirably. The stings are negligible, for one soon becomes inured to them ; and no one knows how mellifluous summer in winter can be that has not eaten keeping pears stewed in honey.

Mr Warburton quickened his pace. They were in the garden now, the lighted house standing on the terrace rose before them, and the statues ranged along the windows were like guests already arrived.

' Are we going in with him ? ' she whispered.

' Let us,' he answered.

The garden was filled with the smell of lilac.

With an unspoken consenting they paused, turned to each other and kissed, forgetting in that darkness the fragrant dusk about them.

THESE were the scenes, the thoughts and the adventures that Sukey recalled, lying quiet in the early morning of the day when her child would be born. A grey light dwelt in the room, and through the chink in the curtains she had watched a star grow suddenly bright and disappear, as a candle flares up before its ending. The starlings conversed with their sliding, watery voices, and the near and far cocks crowed in rivalry. Soon she would hear footsteps tramping down the lane—the heavy boots of the farm men—and the voices of the women going to the well and to the wood-stack. Then would follow the crack of a stick knapped in two for the hearth, the clatter of a bucket, the ring of tinware and crockery, the swift voices of children, the postman's rat-tat, maybe—all the beginning noises of an ordinary day, an ordinary dear day, just such another as the many days to which she had risen with a glad and busy heart. But on this day she would not rise ; and she must even hold back her thoughts from following the concerns of her household : Eric's breakfast, and the kitten, and the dog, and the fowls, and the geraniums on the window-sill.

Mrs Lucy must see to them, while she lay here and remembered.

For there was so much to remember, and it was essential that she should remember it all, once more possessing herself of the past. Not that she feared death—though women die in childbirth; but something told her that she would never again be able to remember as she could remember now. It is the childbed, and not the marriage-bed, that changes women. With the first child is born the mother, a new, a different being, who, even should she seek to do so, can never more re-enter the habitation of her maiden self. For a while yet, in the glimmering room where the clock ticked and the light fingered this and the other, the former Sukey watched with her, a faithful presence, a sister; but even now she was unsure of her tenure: at each pang she covered her face, and at the sound of Mrs Lucy's step on the stairs she hid under the bed; at the child's first cry she would vanish like a ghost at cockcrow.

Shall I ever see you again, Sukey, Sukey Bond? Perhaps when Sukey Seaborn was an old woman, sitting chilly in the sun or stooping among her fruit bushes, Sukey Bond would come back, the last, the truest, the most piteous of her children, innocent of time, wearing her old-fashioned clothes and her unspotted youth, intently offering those dim joys and sorrows, dreams and anxieties, like a wreath of ghost flowers, long ago bleached and whirled to atoms, that only in her hands and to her constant sight retained their living colours. She would come walking across the marsh fields, coming from the orchard, her lips still strange to her from the burden of the first kisses. She would come from another field, where under the weeping snow she had held out her hands to the wolf's sorrow, and from Mrs Oxey's parlour with a blue silk petticoat, and from the Queen's palace with a Bible. 'I love,' she would say.

I love. The maiden can speak thus boldly, and only the maiden, whose love is still their own to proclaim, an intensity cloistered in its own fire, an inviolate astonishment. Already it seemed curious to her, and slightly embarrassing, that she should have spoken so. Never again would her lips utter such brazen boasting. She would say instead : I never saw such a child for tumbles ; Your father always was a one for gooseberry tart ; My mind misgives me that she is sickening for something ; Don't forget to put on the clean shirt ; Wasn't there something else that I meant to order from the grocer ? Did I remember to put the scissors out of reach ?

There 's scarlet fever in the village ; I shall soon need a new thimble ; Eric will come back soaked to the skin ; When I can find the time I must turn out that cupboard ; Don't pull pussy's tail.

I shall be like Mrs Mullein, she thought. I hope I shan't have seven children ; it 's enough to unsettle any man.

' Where 's Eric, Mrs Lucy ? Did he eat his breakfast properly ? '

' Don't you fret yourself about him, my dear. He 's right enough.'

' But where is he ? '

' Somewhere around. Telling the bees, I reckon.'

When the child was older it would have to be kept away from the bees. There was croup, too, and the christening, and its grandmother. For Mrs Seaborn had come back from some place abroad, forgetful of the Princess, smiling and soft-spoken as of old, a dangerous dove. Leaning on Mr Warburton's arm, she had come to visit them, had crumbled a slice of cake and walked through the garden, languid, distant, and unpleased. There had been nothing blooming but the Christmas roses. ' It 's a pity they should come such a bad colour out of doors,' she had said, her whole demeanour pronouncing that the husband of such a creature as Sukey

Bond was no son of hers. That night Eric had cried out in a bad dream.

Thus her thoughts had hastened forward already, borne away by that same tide of living which now, gathering up its strength, laid fierce hold on her, sweeping her beyond sight of all the old landmarks, subduing her to its purpose— to bring forth the living child, another span of years arching from her own, another measure of time to come, a net to catch the future in. And already the maiden Sukey, discarded, covering her face, retreated from the bedside, turning back to her secret dwelling-place among things past : there she would abide, irrecoverable, unassailable, alone with her love. She would need no other companion. . . . Oh, stay, stay ! Let me thank you before you go, faithful one that I must now break faith with, purchaser of this life you cannot share ! Suddenly, as though the maiden Sukey had flown into her bosom for a last embrace, she recaptured the past, and possessed her love in its entirety, and comprehended, as never before, as never again, the vehemence of that single purpose, the stubborn hope that had held out against all.

' Look ! Here is something you had forgotten,' whispered the maiden Sukey. ' I give it back to you now, for a token, for a keepsake.'

When she had gone out by the back door of the rectory into the drizzling snow and the enormous unexpected bulk of the winter night, a kitten, crouching bedraggled on the step, had uttered a loud squeal of delight and rushed indoors, its short legs prancing, its tail stuck straight out behind it. I have not even a kitten, her despair had thought. And now . . .

'If I bear a son,' she said, 'I will call him Sorrow. But if it is a girl child, she shall be called Joy.'

The river ran faster, ran deeper. It was Mrs Lucy's wrist she clung to, not the sphinx's clawed and golden foot. But who was Mrs Lucy, and why was she here? All actuality had reeled away, her pangs had shaken down a universe. 'Joy!' she cried out, not knowing what she spoke.

If you would like to know more about Virago books, write to us
at Ely House, 37 Dover Street, London W1X 4HS for a full
catalogue.

Please send a stamped addressed envelope

VIRAGO
Advisory Group

**Give them
the pleasure of choosing**
Book Tokens can be bought
and exchanged at most
bookshops